SWAMP MONSTER

A Victor Storm Novel

TERRY F. TORREY

Visit terryftorrey.com for a complete list of works by Terry F. Torrey, and subscribe to the newsletter to be notified of promotions, special events, and new releases of things worth reading.

This is a work of fiction. All of the characters, organizations, and events portrayed in this work are ether products of the author's imagination or are used fictitiously.

2024-01-09

CHAPTER ONE

At his seat in the bar, Victor Storm realized that the greasy fries and flat beer in front of him were probably, unfortunately, his dinner. The thought lingered a moment in his brain as his fingers brought another of the large steak fries to his mouth and he chewed it, then washed it down with a swallow of the beer. It was a little after six in the evening. He hadn't eaten since lunch, and he didn't think he was going to eat after this, so this was probably it. Of course, the bar had a full kitchen, and he could order a proper meal. If he was looking to eat or to enjoy himself, however, he'd be across the river in his own neighborhood in St. Louis. Instead, he was here, at a dive bar in East St. Louis. He wasn't here to eat, or even to drink, really. He was looking for trouble.

The bar's name was the Rusty Crown, and it referred to itself as an English pub, and it tried to look the part, with British flag tabletops, busts of kings and queens on the walls, banners of soccer teams on the peaked ceiling, framed maps and pictures of London, and even a suit of armor. The place had a large bar area with tall tables and a long, polished, wooden bar, complete with a surly barman ready to serve drinks. At the end of the bar near the entrance was an area with genuine cork dartboards and chalk scoreboards, and here about eight men of various ages were engaged in what looked like a league. Though the men each held pints of draft beer and laughed a lot, they seemed to take the game seriously.

Victor sat on the opposite side of the bar, where a set of archways led to a dining room with low tables and a fireplace. Victor sat with his back to the wall by the fireplace, and though his first intention had been to watch the dart players, he was distracted by the action in the dining room. A pair of tables in the back of the dining room by the bathrooms had been topped with poker tables, and a group of people were playing in a small tournament. Victor counted a dozen men of a variety of ages and races, plus a balding tournament director who stood to the side with his hands on his hips, watching the action.

What had caught Victor's eye, however, was the girl sitting at a table behind one of the players, positioned so that they could talk. Her hair was either dark blond or very light brown, and though she was sitting sideways to Victor and he couldn't quite see, her eyes seemed to be blue. She looked to be under twenty-one, and maybe she was, because the drink on the table in front of her looked like a cola. She reminded Victor of his daughters, and it was easy to imagine her as one of them in a few years. And that was what had him—despite his training and best effort—scowling in her direction. She wasn't the problem, though. The problem was the dipshit she was talking to.

He was a moron, through and through. He had come in just as the players had lined up and the tournament director had given out stacks of playing chips a half hour earlier. He was a greasy white guy with a mullet that looked dirty blond— and not merely the color, but actually greasy and dirty. His face was blemished and pocked, resembling a reaction to dairy products amplified by an unhealthy lifestyle. He had a dirty blue nylon vest hanging on the back of his chair, and he was wearing blue jeans with a gray sleeveless T-shirt—the kind designed to show off muscles. The shirt did indeed show his arms to be rather muscular, although to Victor it looked more like the man was doing something specifically targeted at his arms rather than a comprehensive fitness and strength program. The man was drinking draft beer, and he was already on his third since the game had started, but he had been a jerk even before the alcohol. He slung insults and rude gestures at the other players. He kept leaning to the side and farting, once loud enough that Victor could hear him across the room. He kept proclaiming himself to be the best player. And in between hands, he turned to talk to the girl who had come in with him. He was a grade-A jerk, but the girl was eating it up, laughing and making eye contact with him, and even shifting in her seat so that he could reach her knee better when he reached back to rest his hand on it.

Victor had seen hundreds of young women more or less just like her in his forty-two years, but there was something special about this particular one: she reminded him of his daughter.

"You want to play?" the tournament director asked Victor. He gestured to the tables, then turned back to Victor with a friendly smile. "We've got plenty of room for you."

Victor shook his head. "I don't know how," he lied.

The tournament director nodded, still smiling. "Nobody knows how before they learn, and this is a great place to get started."

"No, thanks," Victor said. "I'm supposed to be meeting someone."

"We've got room for two," the tournament director said.

Victor gave him a weak smile. "Sorry."

"Okay, well, we're playing Monday this week because it's a holiday," he said, "but we usually play every Tuesday, Thursday, and Sunday at eight o'clock, so feel free to come back if you ever feel like having a good time."

Victor found the man's friendliness annoying, and he felt the urge to punch him in the face, but fortunately, he was already walking back to the game tables, giving Victor a smile back over his shoulder as he walked away.

Victor sighed and tried to turn his attention back to his food and drink. A few of the players had turned to see who the tournament director was inviting to play, and a couple of them were still appraising them. One of them, a pudgy fellow wearing a baseball cap that seemed intended to cover a balding head, nodded in Victor's direction and raised his glass at him. Victor gave him a grim smile. It felt important for some reason for him to establish himself as a serious person in the room.

He scoffed at him, then sighed, raised his glass, and downed the rest of his beer. He'd spent the last hour trying to be unnoticed in the room, almost invisible.

Now he was going to need to try something else.

———

Victor should have left, but he didn't. He should have only had one more beer, too. Another strike.

He couldn't leave, and he couldn't stop drinking. All he *could* do was keep staring at the girl who reminded him of his daughter and wonder what she was doing here with that moron. She seemed like a nice person, and he definitely was not.

This was February, and his daughter Rose was only fifteen. In six months, though, she'd be sixteen, and in only a few years she could be visiting places like this and hanging out with morons like that.

In fact, for all Victor knew, maybe she already was.

She and her younger sister, Victor's other daughter Lynn, lived with their mother, Victor's ex-wife Angelina in North Carolina, and Victor hadn't seen them in many months.

And now his ex-wife was in a relationship with some guy named Larry, and they were living with him, and everything was complicated and he felt like he was dropping the ball somehow.

So, he sat where he was, and tried not to stare at the girl, and tried to figure out something useful to do, and failed all around.

At the top of the hour, the players took a break. While the tournament director changed out the chips on the table, a few of the players stayed in their seats, a few others wandered around the bar, and several headed outside, taking cigarettes and lighters out of their pockets and purses as they did. The moron and the girl got up to go outside as well. However, the moron headed into the bathroom, and the girl went outside with the others.

Victor saw his chance.

Nonchalantly but urgently, he swallowed the last of his beer, then put the glass down and got up to follow the others outside. The tournament director was moving some of the chips from the table into a set of small buckets, and most of the players who had stayed behind had taken out cell phones, and no one paid Victor any attention as he walked between the tables to the back of the room. Victor glanced in the direction of the bathroom doors, which were closed, then pushed open the side door and stepped outside.

The weather was appropriate for February in Illinois, which meant it was cold. The poker players who had stepped out here to smoke had not bothered to put on their coats, and they had their hands jammed in their pockets or crossed in front of themselves to try to keep warm. The girl had been wearing her jacket inside, and she was wearing it now. So was Victor.

Victor stepped outside and sized up the situation. The poker players, a few men and a woman, stood with their backs to the wall of the building, apparently to stay out of the chilly breeze. To Victor's left was the front of the building, where other patrons could sit outside if they were brave enough or desperate enough to smoke. To the right, a dark alley went behind the building, and Victor could see bits of plastic, and he imagined the dumpster must be back there.

The poker players smoked quickly, blowing their smoke up into great clouds in the light over the side door. The young woman stood with them, and Victor was disappointed to see that she, too, was holding a cigarette. He doubted she was eighteen, and he wondered if the moron had helped her get started smoking.

The group had been making small talk, but they stopped and looked at Victor expectantly as he came out after them. The pudgy man with the cap was one of the group, and he nodded at Victor cordially. Victor nodded back.

Victor knew there was no time to waste, and he approached the young woman. In the dim exterior light, she looked even more like his daughter. "Excuse me, Miss," he said to her.

The young woman turned to him, and as she did, the pleasant smile on her face faded immediately. She looked as though she'd been caught by her father.

"Sorry," Victor said. "I didn't mean to startle you."

The young woman continued to be wary of him, and he realized that he was almost literally a stranger in a dark alley.

"Watch out," the pudgy man said to the girl, chuckling. "He looks like a killer." He grinned at Victor.

Victor forced a laugh. "No," he said. "I'm not—" He cut himself off, realizing he had no idea what to say. "I just—"

At that moment, the side door burst open, and the moron stepped outside, lighting a cigarette as he did. He had not bothered to put on his jacket, and the white skin of his arms looked pale in the bleak light outside. "All right, you guys," he said. He exhaled and blew a cloud of smoke at the group. "Make way for the best."

The pudgy man groaned at him and waved the smoke away. "Give it up, Jordan," he said. "We're trying to hear what this man has to say to Melissa."

The moron, whose name seemed to be Jordan, stopped with a start and turned to Victor as though seeing him for the first time. "What?" he said, the smile leaving his face. "You want something with my girl?"

Victor stared at him, trying to find the balance between being merely assertive and looking for a fight. He looked over at the young woman, whose name was apparently Melissa. She now looked as though she was terrified of what might happen. Reluctantly, Victor shook his head to try to defuse the situation. He gave Melissa a smile, then turned back to Jordan. "No," he said with a shrug. "She just reminded me of someone else."

"Oh, she reminded you of someone else, did she?" Jordan said, either misunderstanding the concept or wanting to find it offensive anyway.

"That's what I said," Victor said.

"Is that true?" Jordan asked, turning to Melissa.

Looking a little scared, she nodded, although of course she could have no idea what Victor was thinking.

Jordan turned back to Victor, and he looked as though he

wanted to say something hostile, but before he could, the side door opened again and the tournament director stuck his head out.

"We're six minutes into our five-minute break," he said to the poker players. "We're dealing in here."

The poker players stubbed out their cigarettes on the wall outside the door and filed inside. Jordan gave Victor another dirty look, then wrapped his arm protectively around Melissa as they took a few more drags off their cigarettes.

Victor stood to the side with his hands in his coat pockets. He felt as though he should say something more, but he had no idea what.

After a moment, Melissa stubbed out her cigarette with a delicate gesture, Jordan threw his toward the back alley, and they went back inside. Before they disappeared, Jordan gave Victor one last sneering look.

As the door closed behind them, Victor sighed and shook his head, disappointed in himself. He wanted to go back into the bar, to grab Jordan, and to pin his limbs in various positions that flexed the joints the wrong way until the ligaments experienced damage that would take a few months to heal.

Instead, he did what he thought he probably should have done an hour earlier: He turned on his heel and went back to the bus stop to head back across the river, back home.

CHAPTER TWO

In the dream, Victor is surrounded by people he doesn't know, but they seem familiar to him.

Except for the moron. The moron from the bar is there.

In the dream, however, Victor has known the man for a long time. Long enough for him to be a proven nuisance.

Long enough for Victor to decide to do something about him.

In the dream, there is a flurry of activity. It feels familiar, but Victor doesn't recognize it. People talk and move around. In the commotion, there is an opportunity. The other people move off somewhere, leaving Victor behind. The moron is the last to go.

Victor catches him before he can get away.

From behind, Victor slips a loop of wire around the man's neck and pulls it tight.

The moron struggles and fights. Although the man is younger, and his upper arms bulge, he is no match for Victor and the wire. He barely puts up a fight at all.

Victor twists and tightens the wire. Strangely, though, the man keeps breathing, keeps *living*.

Victor tries to pull the wire tighter, and although the man is utterly unable to fend off Victor and the wire, he keeps on going.

Victor is still struggling with him when the people start to return.

Someone is there. It's the pudgy man. "What's this?" he asks, looking at the moron with the wire around his neck.

"It's nothing," Victor says, letting go of the wire. He tries to let the moron go, now hoping he would just ignore what had happened. "He's all right."

The moron stands stupidly. He pulls at the wire, and Victor sees that it is embedded in a deep groove around his neck.

"What's wrong?" someone else asks.

The pudgy man looks closer at the moron's neck. "I think he tried to kill him," he says.

Victor says nothing. He pushes on the moron's back to try to make sure he is on his feet, then takes a step back himself, hoping everyone else will ignore the moron. Hoping the moron himself will not realize what happened.

It almost works.

The moron stands dumbly in place.

The crowd doesn't seem to notice.

Then the pudgy man steps to look closer, and there is no way he can't see the wire.

Everyone is going to know what Victor has done.

Victor feels cold fear run through his body.

———

Victor woke with his heart beating fast. His mouth felt pasty, but the sheets he lay on and under were soft—softer than his own. And he could feel heat coming from the other side of the bed.

He rolled onto his side and propped himself up on his elbow to get his bearings. No light shined on the window blinds, but a light in another room of the apartment lit this bedroom in a faint glow. He recognized the bed and sheets, the comforter, and the mottled pattern on the carpet as Janine's bedroom. He glanced at the window, where no light pressed on the back of the blinds, and before he even turned toward the alarm clock on the other side of the bed, his body told him that it was five in the morning: time to get up. He sat the rest of the way up, turned, and swung his legs off the bed.

"Good morning," Janine said behind him. "Are you getting up?"

Victor turned to look at the woman in the bed beside him. The blond in her hair stood out in the darkness, but her blue eyes looked dark, almost black. "Yeah," he said.

She groaned. "Why?" she asked. "What do you have to do at this hour?"

Victor shook his head. "After twenty years in the army, my body won't let me sleep past five," he said.

"But you've been retired for a few years, right?" Janine said. "Time to adjust to civilian life."

"I'm trying," Victor said, giving her a smile. He reached over and patted her on the hip. "You go back to sleep."

"What are you going to do?" she asked.

"I think I'll call my daughters," Victor said. "It's six o'clock in North Carolina. I'll talk to them before they go to school."

"Will they be up at this hour?" Janine asked. "I don't remember getting up at six when I was a kid."

"Maybe not," Victor said, "but I need to go get ready to call them anyway." Victor inhaled deeply, thinking about everything else going on. "Plus, I probably need to help Samantha with my parents' stuff."

Janine rolled onto her side and adjusted the pillow under her head. "Will I see you later?"

"I'll be in class tomorrow," Victor said.

"Tomorrow?" Janine said, disappointment in her voice. "Can't you come back later today?"

Victor shrugged. "I don't know," he said. "I'll try."

"You want me to drive you home?" she asked.

"No, thank you," Victor said. "I like the bus."

———

It was still before six in the morning when Victor stepped off the bus at the condominium tower in downtown St. Louis where he lived in the condo that had belonged to his parents, but the horizon had begun to lighten in the distance beyond the black Mississippi River and the city was coming alive.

Although it had been nearly six months since his parents were murdered in Florida, and Victor had been staying in their condo since that time, arriving at the condominium tower still felt more like coming to visit them than coming home. This was his home, though, at least for now. The lease on his former apartment had expired at the end of the year, and though he had at first wanted his sister to take the entirety of his parents' estate, she had insisted that he take half, which included the condo, and he had reluctantly agreed.

Victor took the elevator to the ninth floor, his senses sharpening as he got closer. When the elevator door opened, he looked into the hallway before stepping out and treading softly to the condo's door.

He wasn't being paranoid. He'd been making enemies lately, and he needed to be careful.

Thanks to the oil Victor had applied, the lock and the

hinges made no sound as Victor slipped inside. Without turning on the lights, he padded through every room. Nothing seemed amiss. Finally satisfied, he turned on the lights and returned to the living room.

He took off his coat and hung it on the hooks on the wall behind the front door, then sat on the couch to take off his shoes, and was surprised when the doorbell rang.

Keeping his shoes on, he went to the front door and put his eye to the peephole. A man stood outside, facing the door. The peephole lens distorted the view, but the man appeared to be middle-aged, non-threatening, and alone. Victor took a deep breath, let it out, and opened the door.

"Well, you're up early," the man said. He had a pudgy face, and buck teeth showed when he smiled. He took a clipboard out from under his arm and looked at a document clipped to it. "You're Victor Storm?" he asked.

Victor frowned, thinking of the probate paperwork for his parents' estate. "Yes, but—"

The man took the document off the clipboard and handed it to him with a smile. "Here you go, sir," he said. "You've been served."

Victor took the document and tried to make sense of it. "Are you sure this is right?" he asked. "Samantha has been handling the paperwork."

"Hmm, I don't see a Samantha here," the man said, looking down at what appeared to be a receipt on the clipboard and making a note with a pen. "The plaintiff says 'Angelina Storm.'"

"Angelina?" Victor said, frowning at the full name of his estranged wife. "What is this?"

The man seemed to sense his confusion. "I'm sorry, sir," he said. "It looks like a petition for divorce."

———

"So, first thing this morning I got served these divorce papers," Victor said, shaking his head, "and I tried to call her to find out what's going on, but she won't answer her phone."

"Divorce papers," Lou said. He had dark skin and a deep voice, and he and Victor had been good friends for more than twenty years. "I think that pretty much answers what's going on."

Victor waved a hand. "But ... what is she thinking? That's what I want to know."

"I have to solve cases every day," Lou said. He gave a grim shake of his head. "This one's not complicated. She wants to divide your money and assets."

"Bah," Victor said. "I'm retired military and I practice voluntary simplicity." He frowned. "Plus, I already gave her practically everything we had when she left."

Lou scoffed, then turned serious. "Man, I know it's past time for it," Lou said after a moment, "but I'm sorry to hear it anyway." He tipped his glass of beer in Victor's direction in a salute gesture, then raised it to his mouth and took a drink.

"Past time for it?" Victor repeated, looking surprised. "What?"

Lou lowered his glass and looked sympathetically at his friend. "We've had this discussion before, Vic," he said. "It's going on three years since she left—"

"Not *three* years," Victor said. "Two years and a few months."

"And she's with someone else now, living with him. And you have a girlfriend," Lou said.

"I don't have—It's not—" Victor said. He shook his head again and scoffed in disgust. "We're just *figuring out* what we want to do. We haven't decided yet."

"I'm sorry, Vic," Lou said, "but it sounds like Angie's figured it out."

Victor rolled his eyes and took a long drink of his own beer. They were in Maurice's, a little jazz bar close to the condo in downtown St. Louis. It was a small place, with a long, glossy bar inside the entryway, a line of booths on the other side of the walkway behind the bar stools, a scattering of tables in the room at the end of the walkway, and a stage in the corner around the end of the bar. Victor liked to come to the live shows they had once or twice a week, but today he had wanted to come here because there was no show and it was mostly quiet.

Lou picked up the cigarette pack on the table, shook it, and gave Victor a look of disappointment. "You have another pack?" Lou asked him.

Victor eyed his friend, then reached for his coat pocket and took out a fresh pack. "Of course," he said, "but didn't you quit?"

"Yeah," Lou said, opening the pack, "but when did that ever stop me?"

Victor smiled, took out a cigarette for himself, and handed the pack to Lou. He lit his cigarette, blew the smoke at the ceiling, and handed over the lighter to Lou, who lit his own cigarette and blew the smoke at the waitress's behind as she walked by. The stupid gesture made Victor chuckle. Lou's deep voice suggested a wisdom that contrasted with his juvenile behavior sometimes.

Lou Rollins was an old friend of Victor's. Though they had both grown up in St. Louis, they had not met until they were in basic training in the army. They had been good friends since that time, even though Lou's path had gone through the Military Police to the Criminal Investigation Division and Victor's had taken him through the infantry to the Special Forces. Both had retired after twenty years, but along the way they had met for drinks and adventures in a dozen countries on several continents around the world. After retiring, both had returned to St. Louis, where Lou now worked as a detective for the St. Louis Police Department in the Auto Theft Section.

Victor took another drag off his cigarette. "It's good to be in a civilized place where you can smoke indoors," he said. "The place I was in last night, we had to go outside to smoke like a bunch of kids sneaking around."

"Had to smoke outside?" Lou asked, his expression turning serious. "Were you over in Illinois? Did you go to East St. Louis?"

Victor grunted and waved his hand.

"Damn it, Vic," Lou said in genuine exasperation. "Don't tell me you were out looking for trouble again." He leaned closer to Victor and looked at his head. "You've still got the bruises from last time."

Victor shook his head and leaned back away from Lou's gaze. "What am I supposed to do, *not* give morons what they deserve?"

Lou looked around and lowered his voice. "If you don't go looking for trouble, you won't have to deal with morons in the first place."

"Yeah, well, if anybody was asking for it, this moron was," Victor said. He briefly recounted the actions of the moron at the poker game, playing up how much of a jerk the guy was and how young the young woman probably was, but not mentioning how much she reminded him of his daughter. "But you'll be happy to know that last night I did *not* thump that moron, even though he was asking for it."

"Huh," Lou said, staring at him. "Is the East St. Louis Police Department looking for somebody fitting your description?"

Victor raised his hands in a gesture of surrender. "Not this time," he said. "This time I walked away."

Lou studied him for a moment, scoffed, and took a drink of his beer. "I keep telling you, man, you need to get yourself down to the VA," he said. "Not only could they help you with that PTSD you're always describing but denying, they could also help you get some skills so you could get a job instead of hanging out in bars looking for trouble."

"I don't have PTSD," Victor said.

Lou raised his glass and waggled it at him. "Of course not."

"And I don't need training," Victor continued. "I already *have* a certain set of skills." He frowned at his beer glass. "It seems like I should be able to put them to some good use."

"You mean going bar to bar and fighting every moron on both sides of the Mississippi?" Lou asked. "You really think that will improve the situation of young ladies?"

"I don't know," Victor said. "Maybe."

"Crossing state lines to commit violence," Lou said, as though thinking out loud. "I wonder if that makes it federal."

"Federal?" Victor asked sarcastically. "You think I might be a *national* hero? You think the government might give me another medal?"

Lou laughed.

Victor tried to stand up, but the room was a little more unsteady than he expected, and he sat back down again, hoping Lou hadn't noticed.

He had. "Have you been drinking here all day?" Lou asked, eyeing him.

"All day?" Victor asked. He scoffed at the suggestion and picked up his beer. "Not *all day*. Just since lunch."

"*Lunch?!*" Lou repeated. He looked at his watch. "*Seven hours?!*"

"No, I took an *early* lunch," Victor said. "*And*, I'm just getting started."

"No, Vic," Lou said. "Not this time." He took one last drag

off his cigarette, crushed it out in the ashtray, then tipped back the last of his beer and stood up. Giving Victor a serious look, he put a steady hand on Victor's upper arm. "Let's get you home."

CHAPTER THREE

Victor woke Wednesday morning at five o'clock with his head pounding, his mouth dry, and a feeling of general malaise throughout his body. Taking a hot shower and several painkiller pills did not make everything better, but it took the edge off enough that he could focus on getting things done.

He dressed and went to a nearby diner, where he sat at the counter, watched the crowd fueling their bodies before work, and got some food and coffee going through his own body. And water. Lots of water.

While he ate, he allowed himself to think about the events of the previous day. He knew that Lou was right. Though it surely wasn't easy for Angelina, either, it was probably time for her to move on. It was probably time for him, too. But he didn't like it.

He was more disappointed, though, in his reaction to the bad news. He wanted to cut himself some slack for receiving such a shock in the form of the divorce papers, but that seemed too simplistic. There would always be something in his life to aggravate him, and he had to find some way of handling the stress that didn't involve alcohol, or fighting, or both.

Lou was probably right about that, too.

So, after his food, he stopped thinking. Instead, he went to the nearest bus stop and caught a bus. He tried to keep his attention on the scenery outside the windows as he rode instead of what to expect when he got there, and it mostly worked. It helped that he didn't have far to go.

A short time later, he stepped off the bus in front of the St. Louis VA Hospital.

There, beside the bus stop, he could keep his doubts at bay no longer.

He could see a man entering the facility in a wheelchair.

Another walked up with the gait of a man with a prosthetic leg.

Another, older, veteran walked up wearing tattered clothes and carrying a black garbage bag that might have held everything that he owned.

Watching the scene, Victor realized that these people needed the help available inside. Not him. The people inside might not tell him as much, but they would be thinking it. Everyone would know it.

He didn't belong here. He was fine.

Everybody knew it.

A few minutes later, a bus rolled up to the stop across the street, headed back in the direction Victor had come from.

And when it rolled away, Victor was on it.

———

Wednesday evening, Victor checked the schedule carefully, then took a bus to the St. Louis Community College. Once there, he headed to the humanities building, climbed the stairs to the second floor, and walked down the hallway to his Ethics class. It had been only a week since he had last been here, but given everything that had happened, it felt like much longer.

Since he first started taking philosophy classes here, he'd been having that sensation a lot.

He timed it perfectly. He could hear the instructor, an old philosopher named Garland Chandler, begin talking as Victor approached the door. Chandler looked up at him as he entered, but made no gesture of acknowledgment as Victor tiptoed inside and slipped into his usual seat in the front corner near the door. Janine was sitting in the row behind him. She gave Victor a smile as he sat down, and he tried to return the friendly gesture, but the smile felt grim on his face. Victor glanced around quickly at the others in the room. It appeared to him that some of the students must have dropped the class, but all the ones he had noticed specifically before were still here.

"I have to say," Chandler was saying, "I wasn't sure at first how well my new method of instruction would go." He had iron-gray hair and bushy eyebrows, and he raised them now thoughtfully. "And I'm not sure it's going as well as I'd hoped." On the first day of the ethics class, Chandler had proclaimed the entire academic pursuit entirely fruitless, dropped a stack of potential textbooks into the trash, and had instead opted to give the class an assignment to investigate a case that was in the news, a man named Wyatt Roach, suspected of murdering elderly nursing home patients. The media had taken to calling him the "Angel of Death." Victor's class had debated various ethical aspects of Roach's situation. Despite the outrageous nature of the crimes, it looked as though he might evade prosecution. Less than two weeks early, however, and to everyone's surprise, Roach had leaped to his death from the window of his Kansas City apartment.

No one else in the class or in the world knew it, but Victor had paid a visit to Wyatt Roach, and he had been there when he died. He did not, however, kill him. Not directly, anyway.

"I may think of a better approach later," Chandler continued. "For now, though, we'll try it again for another case."

A murmur went through some of the people in the class. Victor had sensed that the general feeling among his classmates was that the individual case research was a pain, but it was somewhat less of a pain than reading the dry philosophy textbooks and writing papers about them.

"Now, it may be a little morbid to get excited about such things," Chandler said, "but I think our next project may be about to get interesting." His eyes sparkled at the class. He reached into a leather satchel on top of his desk and pulled out a sheaf of stapled papers. "Have any of you heard about Trever Mills?" he asked.

A timid hand went up in the back of the room.

Chandler handed the stack of papers to the woman sitting at the front of the room on the other side from Victor and gestured for her to pass them out, then went back to the desk at the front of the room. "Yes?" he asked, pointing at the person who had raised her hand.

"That guy in Dallas?" the woman said.

Chandler waited expectantly for more.

"That did those things," the woman added.

Chandler continued to wait.

"Isn't he that minister's son?" a person in the middle of the room asked.

Victor recognized the voice and turned to see a thin young man in his early twenties wearing a suit. He had been in the other philosophy class Victor had taken, and his manner of dress made Victor think of him as "Dapper Dan."

Chandler sat on the corner of the desk. "Trever Mills," he said. "Son of televangelist minister Edmond Mills, counselor at the Trinity River Christian Outreach summer camp owned by the church on their property along the Trinity River southeast of Dallas, Texas."

A young black woman sitting in the middle, who was named Loretta and had also been in Victor's previous philosophy class, peeled off one of the papers from the stack and handed the rest to Victor. He took one and handed the stack to Janine.

"The camp has been operating for close to twenty years," Chandler continued, "and Trever Mills was a counselor from the time he was twelve until last year, when he was twenty-two years old and accusations started to become public."

Victor and the rest of the class wondered what accusations, of course, but given the description of the situation so far, it wasn't hard for Victor to guess.

"Last fall," Chandler said, "a pair of victims came forward, two brothers aged ten and twelve, and they said Trever Mills had abused them sexually at the camp."

Someone in the back of the room gasped, which made Victor shake his head.

"They said that Mills had done various things to them, including violating them with a broomstick."

The person in the back of the room gasped again, and several others groaned.

Chandler raised his eyebrows and nodded sympathetically. "Since that time, more kids have come forward with allegations against Trever Mills, and now he has finally been arrested."

"About time," Loretta said.

"What took so long?" Janine asked under her breath, but loud enough for Victor to hear her.

Apparently, Chandler heard her, too. "What took so long seems to have been that Trever Mills's father is a major supporter of the governor and the other major politicians in the state, and the police felt that they had to handle the situation delicately."

Janine scoffed in disgust.

"Now," Chandler said, "this case has a lot of complexity. Mills is in his third year at college, and he intends to start law school after he graduates next year."

Someone scoffed and said, "Good luck."

"He may have been born lucky," Chandler said. "He's a member of one of the most powerful political families in the state."

Victor looked at the paper Chandler had passed out. There was not a lot of detail on it. At the top was the name "Trever Mills." Under that was a section with the heading "Overview" containing a paragraph describing the basic information Chandler had just mentioned: a short biography of Trever Mills, a description of the camp and his family, and the accusations against him. Below that was a section labeled "Chronology" with only a few dated items listed below: when Trever had started as a counselor, when the accusers had come forward, when he had been arrested, and when he was slated to begin law school.

"The District Attorney's office in Dallas has put out a call for any other victims to come forward, as well as anyone else who might know something about this case," Chandler said. "If the evidence supports the claims and Mills is convicted, the repercussions would wreck his future. Even if he didn't get jail time, he'd most likely have to register as a sex offender for life, and his legal career would in all likelihood be a non-starter."

"Serves him right," Dapper Dan said.

"So," Chandler said, rising from the desk and clapping his hands together in front of himself, "regardless of how it develops, this case lets us ask some interesting ethical questions. Does anyone have any suggestions?"

The class went silent for a moment, then a young man sitting in the seat next to Dapper Dan spoke up. His name was Jayson, and most of what he said in the class were jokes. "Is it okay to kill him?"

Several people chuckled.

"Maybe," Chandler said. "You should frame that as an ethical question, and we can explore it."

"That *was* an ethical question," Jayson said. He raised his hands in a framing gesture. "'Is it okay to kill him?'"

"Yes," Loretta said.

Chandler tipped his head with a little smile. "If they were accusing you," he said to Jayson, "would you think it was okay for the answer to be 'yes'?"

"If I did it, sure," Jayson said.

"And you're sure *he* did it?" Chandler asked. "Without a trial or anything?"

Jayson nodded. "Sometimes you can just tell, you know?"

Chandler shook his head. "No, I don't know," he said. He shook his head again and turned to the rest of the class. "Other ethical questions? Anybody?"

They thought for a moment.

"'Is it okay to skip a trial for guilty people?'" Jayson suggested.

Dapper Dan chuckled and shook his head.

"I was hoping for something more substantive," Chandler said, "but that will do."

They wrote it in their notebooks, and the class fell silent again. Janine bit the end of her pen thoughtfully.

"How about: 'Would it be wrong for him to do exactly what he's accused of?'" Victor asked.

Chandler turned to him with a sardonic smile. "Interesting," he said.

The class continued to suggest questions, and Chandler kept helping them to frame the questions as ethical questions and to explain what made them so. It took most of the class a long time to get, but Victor understood the concept from the start. Furthermore, most of the questions the class came up with were straightforward and unimaginative, and Victor grew bored.

Eventually, Chandler moved to wrap things up. "I think we're on the right track now," he said. "I don't have any special homework for this weekend, except I hope you'll research the details of the case and come prepared to evaluate more of the ethical questions next time." He started to turn away, then seemed to remember something and turned back. "Oh, and next time I'll assign you partners for the group project."

Normally, Victor did not like it when people complained about the content of the classes. When the groan went up in the room at the news of the group project, however, his voice joined in the protest.

CHAPTER FOUR

After class, as had become their habit, Victor joined Janine for a drink across the street from the campus at a little place called Tango. It was a small, pleasant cafe that catered to the St. Louis Community College students, specializing in coffee in the mornings, sandwiches at lunchtime, and bottles of beer in the evenings. Janine ordered a beer, and, after a moment, Victor did, too. It was pretty quiet at this time of the evening, and Victor and Janine sat at a table in the back.

"Wow, what a case, right?" Janine said as they sat down.

Victor shrugged. "I wish it was more unusual."

They talked about the case for a while, but they had few details, and the topic quickly petered out.

"You seem quiet tonight," Janine said, then added, "Well, quieter than usual. Something on your mind?"

Victor sipped his beer, looked at her over the top of the bottle, then took another sip. "I got served divorce papers yesterday," he said.

Janine made a grim face. "Did I know you were still married?" she asked.

"Yeah," Victor said. "I *think* so."

Janine nodded. "I remember you said she left a couple of years ago. I guess I just thought ..."

Victor said nothing.

Janine took a drink of her beer, then gave Victor an appraising look. "You didn't know it was coming?" she asked.

Victor shook his head. "No."

"Well, that's pretty big, then," she said. "I'm sorry."

"Thanks," Victor said, not meeting her eyes.

"Is it what you want?" Janine asked.

"Not really," he said. He shook his head in disgust. "It's probably for the best, but I still don't know how to do it, you know?"

"Yeah, I've been through it before, remember?" Janine said with a nod. He reached over and put her hand on his on the table. "If you need any help, just let me know."

Victor met her eyes. "Thanks," he said.

Janine withdrew her hand, and they were quiet for a moment. Victor finished his beer, stood up, and waved the bottle. "I'm going to have another," he said. "You?"

"No," she said. "I have to drive home, and I have to work in the morning."

"I'll get you one anyway," Victor said. "And I'll help you drink it."

———

Victor's sister Samantha called first thing Thursday morning. "I don't mean to sound pushy or anything," she said, "but I want to make arrangements to get the things I'm keeping from Mom and Dad's stuff out of the condo and over here."

Their parents had been murdered the previous year, and they had recently finalized the probate filing for their parents' estate.

They had divided the cashable accounts equally. Samantha was taking ownership of their flower shop business. Victor was keeping their condo and some other business interests. The bulk of their physical possessions were going to be sold by a liquidation company, except for some mementos and other items of special interest that Victor and Samantha had decided to keep. It was these items that Samantha wanted to pick up.

"You don't sound pushy," Victor said. "I think we both want this done."

"Is this weekend good for you?" she asked. "I was going to rent a truck. You don't have any plans, do you?"

Victor had been spending his weekends looking for trouble in East St. Louis and other places, but he wasn't going to tell her about that, probably not ever. "No, sure," he said. "Sounds perfect."

"I'm sorry," she said. "I didn't even ask how you're doing. Are you okay? What have you been doing?"

"Not much," Victor said. "I'm getting divorced. I got served yesterday."

"Oh, Victor, I'm sorry," Samantha said. "I mean, I know it's for the best right now, but still, I know it's hard. Are you okay?"

"I'm okay," Victor said.

————

Victor was hung over again when his sister knocked on his door at ten o'clock Saturday morning. When he opened the door, however, the first thing he saw was the tow-headed smiling face of his three-year-old nephew, Samantha's son Duncan, as he barged into the house and hugged his legs. "Hi, Uncle Bictor!" Duncan said.

"Hi, Duncan," Victor said, enjoying the sensation of a true smile on his face. "How are you today?"

"Fine," Duncan said. "Mommy said there would be boxes here to play with."

Victor laughed. "There are some empty ones in Grandma and Grandpa's bedroom," he said. "Do you know where—?" But Duncan was already gone, trotting into the master bedroom, and Victor turned back to his sister, still smiling.

"Hi, Victor," Samantha said. "I've got the truck. Did you happen to fill up any more of those boxes?"

Victor shook his head, being careful not to move it too quickly or abruptly. "I've been busy," he said. "Besides, most of the stuff is still in the boxes from when we inventoried it," he said. Frowning, he added, "I think most of the rest is big stuff that won't fit into boxes anyway, like the bed and the hutch."

Samantha gave him a look of concern, as though she could sense he was hung over. "Are you sure you don't want to keep their bed?" she asked. "It seems like the king-sized would be better for you."

"The queen-sized guest bed is fine," Victor said, shaking his head gently again. "I wouldn't feel right sleeping in their bed in their house."

"Yeah, that would be hard," Samantha said.

They headed into the master bedroom, where they found Duncan already standing inside one of the empty boxes and trying to turn another upside down on top of him and it. Rows of boxes of linens, clothes, and personal effects were against the walls on both sides of the big bed in the middle, and Victor began moving them to the bed, separating lighter ones for Samantha to carry and heavier ones for himself.

"Did I tell you I gave my notice at the credit union?" Samantha asked.

"What?" Victor asked, genuinely surprised. "No, you didn't

tell me about that. What's going on?" Then, feeling protective of his little sister, he added darkly, "Did something happen?"

"No, nothing like that," she said, and realizing what he meant, added, "*Victor!*" and playfully cuffed him on the arm. "You don't need to be so defensive of me," she said. "I'm a grown woman."

"I know," he said with a warm smile, "but I'm not sorry."

Duncan had gotten the top box arranged so that it was mostly lined up with the bottom box, with him hiding inside, and they could hear him giggling.

"Anyway," she said, turning back and picking up a box with blue and green plush towels inside it, "Everything was fine at the credit union. Dull, but fine. I just think now that I have the flower shop, I want to try my hand at being a small business owner for a while."

"And put Cara out of a job?" he asked. Victor's father had planned to sell the flower shop as part of their retirement move to Florida, but he was killed before either of those things happened. Since then, his assistant, Cara, had been running the place.

"She won't be out of a job. She'll be the assistant like she was before," Samantha said. "I've already talked to her about it, and she thinks it's a great idea. She says it's been a lot of stress and sadness running it since Dad died."

"I suppose so," Victor said. He thought about his sister taking over for his father running the place. "That sounds right," Victor said with a thoughtful nod. "You know, it seems *right*. Right?"

She nodded, eyes glistening a little. "I think so," she said. "Thank you, Victor."

"But I'm still worried for you," he added.

"Yeah," she said, uncertainty in her voice. "Me, too."

There was a rustle of cardboard, and Duncan popped up,

sending the top box flying behind himself. He had his fingers shaped like guns, and he aimed them at his mother and his uncle. "Pew! Pew!" he shouted. "I got you!"

"Ugh!" Victor said, playing along. "I'm done for!" He fell onto the bed, and all three of them laughed.

CHAPTER FIVE

Saturday evening, Victor had dinner with Janine at her place. She made them a simple meal of spaghetti, a tossed salad, and fresh breadsticks. Victor brought a bottle of wine.

"It looks good," Janine said, taking the bottle and examining the label when he handed it to her.

Victor chuckled as he took off his coat. "It was the first bottle I found in the color and price range I was looking for," he said. "I don't know anything about wine."

Janine looked up at him with a smile. "I'm sure it will be perfect."

It was not.

Janine fixed them plates of steaming spaghetti and sauce, and they dished themselves bowls of salad, sat down, and dug in.

The food tasted excellent to Victor, but when he sniffed the glass he made a face, and when he tasted it, it got worse. "Um," he said. "Kind of like vinegar."

Janine laughed. "Vinegar isn't terrible," she said. "I'm sure it's not that bad."

Victor sniffed at it again and recoiled at the smell. "Try it," he said.

She gave it a confident taste, but immediately shuddered. "Oh, no," she said.

"Told you," Victor said.

Janine took the wine bottle off to the kitchen and brought them glasses of water instead, and they resumed their meal.

Victor found his mind wandering, and though he worried he was being rude, he couldn't help himself. He had realized that he was about ten years older than Janine, and that reminded him of how that moron at the Rusty Crown had appeared to be so much older than the girl he was hanging out with. He was wondering if he was being hypocritical.

"You look like you have a lot on your mind," Janine said after a while.

"Um, yeah, I guess so," Victor said.

"About your divorce?"

"Not really," Victor said. "Well, in a way, I guess."

"We don't have to talk about it if you don't want to," Janine said.

"No, it's not ... bad," Victor said. "I'm just kind of thinking about my daughters. I worry about how they might turn out."

"You mean if you aren't there when they grow up?" she asked.

Victor nodded. He felt shocked by her words, and she must have seen it on his face.

"I'm sorry," she said.

"No, it's okay," Victor said, shaking his head as though to get the fog out. He looked at her with a little smile. "You're a girl, right?" he asked.

"Last time I checked."

He chuckled. "Last time *I* checked, too," he said. "So maybe you can tell me: if you were interested in a guy, but your father didn't like him, would you have stopped seeing him?"

"Now?" she asked. "Or when I was a teenager?"

"When you were a teenager."

She scoffed. "When I was a teenager?" She shook her head. "Good luck with that."

"So, if he was a bad guy, and your father warned you, that wouldn't have mattered?"

"A bad guy?" she asked.

"You know, the kind of guy who isn't going to amount to anything, who's going to run off if she gets pregnant."

She was still shaking her head. "I don't know, Victor," she said. "But I'm wondering: how do you even *know* that he's not a good guy? Would it be right for a father to make that judgment at all?"

"That sounds like one of Chandler's questions from our class," Victor said.

She smiled. "It does at that."

Victor sighed. "I don't know," he said, "but if a father can't influence his daughter when it comes to bad guys, what's he there for at all?"

"How old are your daughters?" Janine asked.

"They'll be sixteen and ten this year," Victor said.

"Sixteen and ten," she repeated thoughtfully. "I can see why this is on your mind."

Victor thought about the young woman at the English pub and gave Janine a grim smile. "Yeah," he said. "I feel like I should be able to do something."

She gave him a thoughtful frown. "Does your daughter currently have a bad-guy boyfriend?" she asked.

Victor shook his head. "Not that I know of."

"Okay," Janine said. "So we've got time to figure it out."

"Do you think it might work?" he asked.

"If my father had cared enough to make a fool of himself for me," she said, "I like to think I would have listened."

————

Sunday evening, Victor got back on the bus and went back across the river to East St. Louis. Lou would not be happy, Victor thought, but Lou would never know.

Probably.

It was a straight shot down the bus line to the Rusty Crown. That was good, because it was a cold night, and he didn't want to have to wait at a bus stop to change buses. The bar was, however, most of the way to the end of the line, which took the better part of an hour. That was fine, because Victor could use the time to think about what Janine had said. He wondered what he might say to the young woman—he remembered that her name was Melissa—or even if he might decide not to say anything at all. It occurred to him that he had been drinking that night, and it was certainly possible that his judgment had been too harsh.

Along the way, many people got on and off the bus. Victor was a little surprised at how busy the bus was for a Sunday evening, but he thought that perhaps it was because the bus was operating on its Sunday schedule—every half hour instead of the weekday schedule of every fifteen minutes.

Finally, the bus approached the stop near the pub and Victor stood up to get off. A couple of other people stood to get off with him, and they all adjusted their coats to prepare for the cold. One of the passengers was a thin old woman wearing gloves, and another was a young man wearing a yellow knit cap. Victor felt a brief pang of jealousy that he had not thought to bring a hat or gloves for himself.

When the bus reached the stop, Victor stepped off first,

stuffed his hands into his coat pockets, and headed down the sidewalk to the bar.

It was about eight-forty-five. The tournament director had told Victor the game would start at eight, so Victor thought he could arrive unnoticed. The bar was on this side of the street, and as he approached, he'd be facing the side with the door the players stepped outside to smoke.

As he drew near, he slowed. He could see the flat brown color of the side of the building, and he could see that no one stood outside the side entry door. The front patio had electric heaters, however, and a few hardy souls sat bundled up and smoking at the outside tables. None of them appeared to be one of the poker players he'd seen before.

Suddenly, he was startled as someone walked past him on the sidewalk, coming up from behind him. He had been absorbed in his thoughts, and he hadn't noticed that someone was close to him. It didn't seem dangerous, but he stepped to the side to make room for the person to pass anyway, and as the man passed, he saw it was the young man with the yellow knit cap on the bus. Victor caught the scent of marijuana as the man passed.

Because they were close to the bar, Victor slowed a little more and let the young man walk ahead of him. The man walked briskly with his hands in his pocket, and when he reached the front entrance of the bar, he turned and crossed the patio to the door. He glanced back at Victor as he pulled the handle, then he disappeared inside.

Victor walked the rest of the way to the bar. There was a window on the front of the bar at the near end of the patio, and it looked to Victor as though it would be facing into the dining room. Looking through it as he passed, Victor noted that he could indeed see into the dining room through the window. Now, he had a plan.

He took his pack of cigarettes out of his coat pocket and lit one as he stepped onto the patio. He gave a quick nod to the people sitting under the electric heater at the other end of the patio, then moved down to stand where he could see in through the window. Fortunately, there was an electric heater positioned there as well, and it wasn't too terrible. And, happily, he found that he had a good view of the poker tables at the far end of the dining room.

To his surprise, the young man with the yellow knit cap walked into the dining room and went down to the poker tables. The tournament director saw him coming and gave him a big smile, then reached into a metal box on one of the dining tables, took out a stack of poker chips, handed it to him, and pointed him toward the table where that moron Jordan had been sitting before.

He wasn't at that table tonight, however. Victor spotted him at the table on the left, and again Melissa was sitting in a seat at a table behind him. Jordan gave the new guy a happy wave, and the new guy sat down to play.

Victor wondered briefly if the people inside could see him through the window. There were some lights on the patio, but it seemed much darker outside than inside, and he was pretty sure they couldn't see him well, if they could see him at all.

At the tables inside, it looked like all the same players from the night before were there. The pudgy man looked like he was wearing the same baseball cap and sitting in the same spot at the table on the left where Jordan was sitting.

Victor smoked his cigarette and watched the scene for a few minutes. Jordan was wearing a sleeveless T-shirt as before, and it looked to Victor like he was up to his usual antics, though it was hard to be sure without being able to hear him. Melissa, however, seemed no less enthralled.

A black-haired waitress came into the room from a door in

the back, spotted the new guy, and went over to him. She left and came back in a minute carrying a glass of beer that she handed to him. The young man said something to her as she did, and suddenly the waitress looked at the window in Victor's direction. She said something back to him, and he turned and pointed through the window straight at Victor.

Victor stepped quickly out of sight to the side of the window, but not before seeing many of the other players and even the tournament director turning to look in his direction.

Without waiting to see what it was about, Victor turned and walked away as briskly as he could without drawing attention to himself. He crossed the street a short way down the sidewalk, then stepped behind the bus stop on the other side of the street and looked back at the bar. The black-haired waitress stepped out the front door onto the patio, looked around, and went back inside.

Victor, feeling out of breath and strangely out of ideas, waited where he was, in the cold.

And a few minutes later, when the next bus came by, headed back to downtown St. Louis, he got on it.

CHAPTER SIX

"So," Chandler said, clapping his hands together in front of himself at the start of the Ethics class on Monday, "what did you find out over the weekend?"

Victor had arrived early to Monday's Ethics class. His brain found something about the case compelling, and he didn't want to miss any information. He had completely forgotten, however, that Chandler had told them to research more details over the weekend, and now he had to fight the urge to slump down in his seat.

"A lot of kids coming forward," Janine said.

Victor was surprised, because the topic had not come up when he'd seen her on Saturday night.

"A lot of boys," Dapper Dan said, and added, "Pervert."

"Would it be less offensive if they were girls?" Janine asked.

"A good question," Chandler said.

"There was one girl," Loretta said.

"At least one," Jayson said, "but not at the camp, so they were saying her case might not be connected."

Janine turned on him. "So they believe the boys, but they don't believe the girl?"

Jayson looked surprised at her. "I don't know," he said. "It's just what I read."

"So most or all of these victims were at the same place," Chandler asked, in a way that suggested he already knew the answer.

"At that church camp," Loretta said.

"Started by his father," Dapper Dan said, and added quietly, "Pervert."

"Down in the swampland by the Trinity River," Jayson added.

"I find it hard to believe that the people at the camp didn't know anything before this," Janine said. "Now that the kids are coming forward, it turns out they had a nickname for Trever there."

"'Swamp monster'," Jayson said.

Many people in the room groaned in disgust.

"So you're telling me that the kids knew what was going on," Janine said, "and none of the other adults there ever heard a whisper?"

"Unbelievable," Loretta said.

"Such a complicated situation," Chandler said. "What ethical questions can we ask here?"

"If there is a god," Victor asked, "why would he let little boys be harmed like this? Is he not truly good, or not truly powerful, or what?"

"A fascinating question with a long history," Chandler said. "Unfortunately, however, not really an ethics question."

"Things like this prove there's a God," Dapper Dan said, and Victor saw that he was talking without looking up from the chair's writing surface. "Because this is the work of the Devil, and if there's a Devil, there has to be a God."

"Another philosophical discussion with a long history," Chandler said, "but, still, not exactly an ethical question."

"How about this," Janine said. "'Should the adults have intervened earlier?'"

"Good," Chandler said, though the murmur in the class suggested no one doubted the answer.

"How about: 'If the kids knew, and they didn't say anything, are they partly to blame?'" Victor asked.

"Don't blame the victims," Loretta said.

"But if the other adults heard about it, and they didn't do anything, they are partly to blame, right?" Victor asked.

"Of course," Jayson said.

"But not if they were kids?" Victor asked. "Meaning, I guess, just under eighteen?"

"Leave the kids alone," Dapper Dan said. "What's wrong with you?"

"I'm just asking questions," Victor said to Dapper Dan. He turned to Chandler. "Isn't that what we're supposed to be doing?"

"It is," Chandler said. "How can we find answers to questions if we don't even dare to ask them?"

"Some questions don't have to be asked," Dapper Dan said. "Everybody already knows the answer."

"If people already know the answer," Chandler said, "it should be easy for them to identify assumptions that we all agree are true, then show how they logically combine to support that an ethical conclusion must also be true."

The class was silent, thinking about that.

"In fact, that will be the project that we'll be working on for the next part of this class," Chandler said.

Someone toward the back of the room groaned, and Victor shook his head in disgust at that person. It always bothered him that people didn't want to do the classwork. They were *paying money* for these classes. It made no sense to pay for something, only to complain about getting exactly what they were promised.

Chandler moved around his desk and took a paper out of his leather satchel, then looked back at the clock on the wall behind him at the front of the room. For a moment, Victor thought they might be getting out of the class early, but Chandler turned back to them and sat on the corner of the desk, clearly ready for a new angle. "As you probably know," he said, "the St. Louis Community College requires most of its classes to have a group project for some reason."

Someone in the area of Jayson groaned loudly, and even Victor had trouble containing his displeasure.

Chandler made a face. "I think this will be a good time for it. For this project, you'll be doing what I just described: taking an ethical question, then attempting to identify necessarily true assumptions that can be logically combined to support an answer to the ethical question. That process can be hard to grasp at first, so it will be good for you to pair up and be able to get assistance from a partner. The two of you will work together on the project, and you'll present your work starting two weeks from tonight, the week before Spring Break."

That might not be so bad, Victor thought. "Do we get to choose our partners?" he asked Chandler.

"Not this time," Chandler said. "I find that when students select their own partners, they tend to keep going back to what's been comfortable for them before, and they miss out on other learning opportunities. So, for this, I've arranged you into pairs that I think will allow you to not only learn from each other but also to complement and support each other."

This time, despite his strong feelings on the matter, it was all Victor could do to keep from groaning out loud at this news.

It seemed like everyone else, however, did express their displeasure in a loud groan.

"Everyone, please, act like adults," Chandler said. "Surely you can handle working with another person on a brief project, and I have a feeling you're going to like these assignments anyway."

Victor looked back at Janine and gave her a hopeful smile. Perhaps there was still some hope.

"Janine Callahan," Chandler said, reading off the list on his paper. "You'll be with Loretta Clay."

Victor gave Janine a resigned look, but she was already smiling at Loretta.

Chandler read off a few more pairs, then announced, "And finally, Victor Storm, you'll be with Daniel Turner."

Victor looked confused at first, not knowing who that was. A *tsk* from the center of the room drew his attention, however, and turning, he recognized who was his partner: Dapper Dan.

Dapper Dan didn't look at him, instead turning to talk to Jayson in what looked like a complaint.

Victor was unable to keep from shaking his head in disgust.

"So, next time," Chandler said, "we'll be finalizing our ethical questions and selecting ones for your group projects."

"And with all these victims coming forward," Janine said, "maybe he'll be convicted by then."

"Or not," Chandler said, looking at her with interest. "Have any of you heard the latest news on this case, as of today?"

No one had.

"Trever Mills's father has hired Lester Dawson to defend him."

"Who's that?" Loretta asked.

"He's a defense attorney widely considered to be an all-star," Chandler said. "He's never lost a case."

After class, Victor again went to Tango with Janine for a drink, and again she had to work in the morning, so it was just a quick one. She offered to take him home afterward, but he wanted to take the bus. He could drive just fine, and he didn't need anyone to give him rides; he took the bus because he *liked* taking the bus.

On the bus, Victor looked out the window on the way home, thinking about Trever Mills in Dallas and Melissa at the English pub. Sometimes, the random things he saw outside the bus would give him a new perspective or fresh ideas about his problems, but this time, nothing sparked his imagination. He did, however, get the idea to get off the bus a stop early and pick up a six-pack of beer at the convenience store.

Back up in the condo, he took a bottle out of the carrier, twisted it open, and put the rest in the refrigerator. He felt restless. Everything was nagging at him, and he didn't know what was the right thing to do.

But he did know he *could* do something.

In fact, he might be the only person who could.

And, he had the sense that he *should*.

He took his beer and his pack of cigarettes out onto the balcony, where two chairs sat facing east with a side table between them. Victor lit a cigarette and sat down in the chair farthest from the door, where he could see the view to the east and also into the condo. The seat was cold at first, but it warmed quickly as he settled into it.

He stared off at the view and sipped his beer, steeped in thought. He tended to muse a lot about the universe and his place in it, but he recognized his level of thinking as very deep, even for him. The Mississippi River, of course, was the Missouri state line, so most of his view lay in Illinois. In the near distance, he could see the river, its black waters glittering with the lights from the bridge above it and the river boats and barges on its surface. Past the river, he could see the twinkling lights of East St. Louis, and in the far distance, he could make out the ridge of black hills against the sky.

Though his mind was preoccupied with the case from his Ethics class, thoughts of that young woman at the English pub kept creeping in.

None of it was any good, and he seemed to already know that he was being pulled inevitably down a path.

He considered what he might do if anyone ever dared to assault his nephew Duncan the way Trever Mills had assaulted those boys. Would he carry out the justice swiftly, himself? And if he did, how would that impact Duncan? He probably couldn't tell him. Would Duncan grow up happy knowing that the person who had violated him had mysteriously disappeared? Or would he be haunted by it?

He thought about what he might do to keep morons like that Jordan guy away from his daughter. He wondered if that problem was unlikely, likely, or even, maybe, already certain. If the situation did present itself—if his daughter did get into a relationship with a loathsome, dead-end human being—and he intervened to drive the guy away, would she be happy about that, or would she be angry, perhaps forever? And even if she were, would getting rid of the moron be worth it for him to pay the price of her anger at him? Maybe, he thought.

Most importantly, he wondered why he should *not* at least *try* to do something in these cases. After all, when he was eighteen, hadn't he taken an oath to (more or less) protect the citizens of this country? Hadn't the army given him a set of skills to uphold that oath? Lots and lots of people had the motive, but Who else had the means and the opportunity to do something good in these situations?

And if the roles were reversed, and someone else had the skills to protect Duncan or his daughter, wouldn't he want that person to use his or her skills to make the right thing happen, whatever that was?

Yes, he would.

So, was the right thing to do here to use his skills to protect the innocent?

Yes, it was.

And that was another weird angle. Maybe few people had the skills to *successfully* intervene in situations like this, but surely lots of people had the ability to *try*.

So why didn't they?

He took a drink from his beer and narrowed his eyes at Illinois.

Because they were scared.

Was *he* scared?

Thinking about that, he took one last drag off his cigarette, then stubbed it out in the ashtray. Straightening, he steadied his gaze across the river again.

Yes, he was scared.

He was scared of making mistakes, of getting caught.

But he was even more scared of disappointing himself and letting everybody down by not doing the right thing.

And the right thing to do was to make sure that these situations had the right outcomes.

So with a tip of his beer like a salute to the Ether, that's what he decided to do.

First, though, he was going to have a few more cigarettes and finish those beers.

CHAPTER SEVEN

Victor went to sleep Monday night feeling powerful, determined, and confident.

He woke up Tuesday morning feeling foolish and doubting himself. And his stomach was unhappy with him.

Mid-morning, Samantha came by in her car. They had already taken the large furniture in the truck she'd rented the previous week, but there were quite a few more boxes to go.

Nonetheless, Victor was surprised to see her on a Tuesday morning. "You don't have to work today?" he asked, as Duncan pushed open the front door, hugged his legs, and went tearing through the condo.

She shook her head with a bright smile. "Didn't I tell you?" she asked. "After I gave my notice, they let me go. They said I was a security concern." She said it as though it were a compliment.

"So, they just fired you?" Victor asked with a frown.

"I guess so," Samantha said, "but they *did* pay me for the rest of the two weeks."

"Cool," Victor said.

"I know, right?" Samantha said. "So now I'm the new manager at the flower shop."

"Owner/manager," Victor said. "Sweet." He gave her a dubious look. "Then, shouldn't you be at work today?"

"Yes," she said, "but I gave myself some time off this morning to pick up some more of these boxes."

"Sweet," Victor said.

They set to work taking boxes down to her car, and while they did, Duncan was a whirlwind of nonstop action, which was mostly playing cop or soldier or something and shooting Victor with his finger-gun. *Pew! Pew!*

As they loaded the boxes, Duncan's presence of course pushed Victor's thoughts back to those of the previous night. By the time Samantha drove away, Victor was feeling again like he had to do something, probably.

The first thing he had to do was to meet Lou for lunch.

———

"Sounds good," Lou said when Victor called asking to meet him. "I'm working a case, and there's a diner that will be perfect."

Lou gave Victor the address, and it turned out to be a ten-minute walk away, faster to walk than to take the bus. The restaurant turned out to be a twenty-four-hour place that specialized in breakfast food, and it smelled like hash browns and sausage when Victor walked in. Lou was already at a booth by the window facing the street, and he spotted Victor and waved him over as soon as he walked in. He had a cup of coffee in front of him and a toothpick in his mouth.

"We got word there's a chop shop operating out of that warehouse," Lou said, taking the toothpick out of his mouth and pointing it at the bottom floor of a large, black, nondescript building across the street. "I'm watching it for a while to see what kind of traffic it gets." He put the toothpick back into his mouth. "If any."

"Haven't seen anything yet?" Victor asked.

"No," Lou said, sounding dejected, "but at least we can have a nice lunch and I can put it on my expense report."

"Mine, too?" Victor asked.

"Of course," Lou said. "You'll be watching the place for me while I'm in the can."

Victor chuckled. "Anything going on over there?" he asked.

"No," Lou said. "Haven't seen anything all day."

"Maybe something happened when you were in the can," Victor said.

"Maybe," Lou said, raising his eyebrows at him with a serious look. "That's why I need you here."

Lou had already ordered, but he flagged down a brown-haired waitress in a forest green uniform and she brought some coffee and a menu for Victor, and he ordered a simple burger and fries.

"So, what's on your mind?" Lou asked after the waitress had left. "I hope you've been staying out of trouble in East St. Louis." He scoffed. "And everywhere else would be nice, too."

"I haven't touched that moron across the river," Victor said. "Although, to be honest, I think I should."

"Here we go," Lou said, shaking his head in disgust. "You don't need to do that, Vic. A guy like that is going to run into trouble everywhere he goes, and it's just a matter of time before he gets himself arrested or some idiot takes real offense and beats him down." He gave him a stern look. "You don't need to be that idiot. It's a problem that creates its own solution."

"I hear you," Victor said. He sighed and tried to let it go, but couldn't. "But why *should* it be someone else? I mean, someone else might have the guts to put him in his place, but not have the proper skills." He shook his head, scowling. "Someone else might get hurt, because what? Because I'm too good to take chances?"

Lou groaned. "Someone else should do it because it will just be a fight, no big deal," he said. "If you do it, it will be an annihilation, and you could get into some serious trouble." He took the toothpick out of his mouth again and waved it for emphasis. "And what would you tell the judge? That you had to do it because you thought he was too much of a jerk for the girl he was with? How far do you think that would get you?"

Victor took a drink of his coffee, and they both turned their attention back out the window at the nothing going on across the street. "You're right, Lou," Victor said after a moment. "Of course you're right. That's exactly why it's bothering me."

Lou grunted. "Just let it go, Vic."

The waitress came back with two plates of the food Lou had ordered: a big steak on one and a large portion of mashed potatoes with the skin still on them on the other. Lou applied generous amounts of steak sauce to the first place, butter to the second, and salt to both, then dug in with a fork and a steak knife.

Victor looked at Lou's food with a smile. "Steak for a stakeout, huh?"

"You got it," Lou said with a chuckle. "When the city's buying ..."

The waitress was back in a moment with Victor's burger and fries, and he set about adding generous amounts of ketchup and pepper.

"Are you still taking that philosophy class?" Lou asked him between bites of steak. "Didn't you say that would help you figure things out?"

"Yes, and that was the idea, but it hasn't helped much so far," Victor said. "In fact, we've pretty much just been talking about current events." While they ate their lunch, he filled Lou in on the information about the Mills case. Victor was used to seeing people have strong reactions to the sordid details of the allegations, but Lou had been in law enforcement for over twenty years, and little surprised him anymore.

"When the stuff was first coming to light," Victor said at the end, "we were pretty sure Mills was looking at a long time in prison."

Lou nodded and made a face. "His father's a wealthy political donor, but that only goes so far."

Victor took a bite of his burger. It was surprisingly good. "You don't think he'll get off?"

Lou shook his head. "They might go easier on him, but the district attorneys in Texas are appointed by the governor, and an elected official doesn't want something like this hanging over him." He cut off a bite of steak and forked it into his mouth. "That asshole's looking at some hard time."

Victor took another bite, thinking. "His father hired Zachery Hooper," he said. "You don't think that will help?"

Lou snorted. "Of course," he said. "That's what the rich people always do: bring in a hired gun to handle their problems."

"You think it will help?" Victor asked.

Lou shrugged and shook his head. "That big shot might get him a deal that shaves off a few years, but he's probably just after the fat check from Trever's father."

Victor considered this. He'd been concerned, but his friend had much more experience with criminal cases than Victor ever wanted to have, and Victor trusted his judgment.

As they finished their food, nothing continued to happen at the building across the street, and their conversation changed to lighter topics. When they were done, Victor had a cup of coffee, they smoked a couple of Victor's cigarettes, and Victor decided it was time to go.

Before Victor left, Lou gave with a concerned look. "How are you doing?"

Victor knew what he meant. "Fine," he said. He tried to make eye contact with a smile, but could manage only the eye contact, and that only for an instant.

"You haven't been hanging out over in East St. Louis, have you?" Lou asked. "At that bar with the poker?"

"*Hanging out* there?" Victor said. "No."

Lou gave him a hard look and shook his head. "One of these days, Vic, you're going to get into some real trouble," he said. "You know that, right?"

Victor scoffed. "I'm flattered that you're worried about me." He stood up, straightened his coat, and put the pack of cigarettes into his pocket.

"Let me have another one of those before you go," Lou said.

With a wry smile, Victor took the pack out of his pocket and shook a cigarette out for him.

"I'm worried about your *daughters*," Lou said, taking the cigarette and pointing it at him for effect. "If they had to grow up without a father ...." He left the sentence unfinished, but the message was clear.

Any trace of a smile left Victor's face, and he straightened and stuck his hand into his coat pockets. "They're *already* growing up without a father," he said. "Thanks for the food. I have to go."

———

Though it was Tuesday and his class was only on Mondays and Wednesdays, when Victor left the diner with Lou, he walked to a bus stop and took a bus to the St. Louis Community College campus. Along the way, he considered what he'd learned from visiting Lou. Victor had been worried about two problems: the moron at the poker place, who he was afraid would ruin the life of the girl who reminded him of his daughter, and Trever Mills, so he was concerned might not get what he deserved. Lou had argued that these two situations would work out well on their own. Victor wanted to believe that, but, watching the city scroll past the bus, with winter still dominating the scene and spring seeming a long way off, Victor found it hard to be optimistic.

That's not why he was going to the campus, however. The syllabus for his class indicated that Chandler had office hours on Tuesday afternoons, and Victor wanted to talk to him.

After Victor rode the bus to campus, walked to the administrative building, and climbed to the third floor, however, he found that Chandler was not in his office.

"He hasn't come back from lunch," the student worker said with a shrug. "You can wait if you want. He *usually* comes back."

Victor did not want to wait, and he had a hunch about where he might be. He exited the administrative building and went across the street to Tango, and there he found Chandler, sitting at a table in the back of the room. He had a stack of papers on the table in front of him, and he was reading the one on top, occasionally making marks with a red pen. Two beer bottles sat on the table with the papers.

Victor walked over to Chandler and cleared his throat. "Good afternoon," he said.

Chandler looked up, recognized him, and nodded with a grim smile. "Afternoon," he said.

"I was hoping to have a quick word with you," Victor said.

Chandler picked up his beer bottle and waved it at the papers. "I'm busy right now," he said. "Come to my office during office hours."

"According to the syllabus, this *is* office hours," Victor said, "and if an office is defined as a room where a person goes to do work, then ..." He gestured at the papers.

Chandler took a drink of the beer, appraising him. "Very well," he said, putting the beer down on the table, "but make it quick."

"It's about the group assignment," Victor said.

Chandler shook his head. "That's a requirement of the accreditation of the class, for some goddamn reason," he said. "It has to be done."

"I don't have a problem with the assignment," Victor said. "I'm just hoping I can get a different partner."

Chandler frowned at him. "Who's your partner now?"

"It's Da—" Victor cut himself off before he could use his nickname, which probably wouldn't gain him favor. "Dan Turner," he said. "But I was hoping I could switch and work with Janine Callahan."

"Who's her partner?"

"Loretta Clay," Victor said.

"And have you discussed this with them?" Chandler asked.

"No, but I'm sure—"

Chandler was already shaking his head. "No," he said, as if the head shaking was unclear. "I assigned the groups for a reason."

"Yes, but—"

"You're a stern-looking, serious guy," Chandler said. "I'm afraid you would intimidate Ms. Clay, and I think Ms. Callahan will be a better fit with her. She's not so ... intense."

Victor thought this sounded right, but he opened his mouth to complain anyway.

"And Mr. Turner is the opposite," Chandler said, cutting him off before he even got started. "I'm *hoping* you'll be able to influence him a bit, otherwise his report will just be Genesis this and Leviticus that."

"But that's—" Victor started, but Chandler was already holding up a hand.

"The decision is final, and I don't have time to talk about it," he said. He gestured at the papers on the table, then reached for the beer and took another quick drink. "Besides," he said. "It's only this one assignment." He put the beer down with a thoughtful frown and added, "So far, anyway."

CHAPTER EIGHT

"One interesting and unique ethical aspect of this case that we haven't talked about," Chandler said, "is the parents."

The class looked at him. It was Wednesday evening, and Chandler had just made his notes on attendance. Victor looked around the room, seeing only looks of confusion.

"How do parents make anything unique?" Jayson asked. "Everybody has parents."

"That's true," Chandler said. "How do the parents in this situation change things?"

Murmurs went through the class as people got ideas and worked up their courage. Looking around, Victor realized there were about a dozen people in the class, though he tended to notice only a handful of them. Someone had arrived early and put an apple on the desk at the front of the room. Chandler had ignored it to this point, but now he picked it up and studied it while he waited for an answer.

"Well, Trever Mills's father is a rich guy who's friends with all the big politicians," said a person in the back, a girl slumped down in her seat and drawing in a notebook.

"So he's probably going to get off," said a kid in the seat beside her. They nodded together as though they were friends.

"I hope not," Janine said, under her breath.

"Should Trever's parents bear some responsibility for his actions?" Chandler asked, raising his eyebrows, but not taking his eyes off the apple.

"If they get him off, they should," Jayson said.

"His father *did* build the camp in the first place," Victor said. "Part of his church."

"It's not the church's fault," Dapper Dan said.

"Couldn't it be said, no matter how children behave, that they were raised to behave that way? Doesn't that seem *necessarily* true?" Chandler asked. "And if it is, should they bear some responsibility for that child's actions, possibly even when he or she is an adult?"

"My parents have no control over me," Jayson said. "They tried, though."

"If your parents raised you to be good, then you need to be good," Loretta said, "but not everybody does that."

Chandler lowered the apple and tipped his head at her. "If a child is doing bad things, but the parents didn't raise her to do bad things, then who did?"

"Someone else," Loretta said.

Chandler smiled. "Then shouldn't the parents be responsible for letting *that* person raise their child to do bad things?"

Loretta shook her head and crossed her arms. "No."

Chandler thought for a moment, turning his eyes back to the apple and rolling it over in his fingers. "If Trever's parents are able to get the charges against him reduced or dismissed," he asked, "what will that mean for the victims, for society at large?"

Practically everyone in the room groaned in displeasure at the thought.

"A travesty," Victor said.

"Well," Chandler said, putting the apple back down on the desk, "let's hope that doesn't happen."

———

After class, Victor again and Janine again went to Tango. Janine ordered a beer, so Victor did also, then Janine led the way to a table in the back. The table they usually sat at was occupied, so Janine sat at a different one, and when Victor joined her, he noted with a smile that it was the one Chandler had been sitting at the previous afternoon.

Victor pulled out the chair and joined her at the table. As he did, he noted that she seemed concerned about something. He had thought she was merely tired before, but now he could tell that it was more. "Something on your mind?" he asked.

She smiled at him. "Is it obvious?"

He returned her smile, then tipped his beer at her in a *cheers* gesture.

She took a deep breath and blew it out, then took a long drink of her beer. "I've been thinking about your divorce," she said.

That surprised him, and he let it show on his face. "My divorce?" he asked. "I wasn't aware that interested anybody but me."

"Well," she said. "I don't mean to pry, or to be needy or pushy or anything like that—"

"So far, so good," Victor said.

"But I wonder how this will change things," she said. "I mean, I like spending time with you."

"I like spending time with you, too," Victor said. "You're a good friend."

Janine scoffed. *"Friend,"* she repeated, considering the word. "Yeah, I hope so."

Victor smiled and tipped his beer at her again. "It's true."

She took another, somewhat smaller, sip of her beer. "And I guess I don't want that to change," she said.

Now Victor tipped his head. "Why would it?"

"Well, your daughters might come," she said. She met his eyes for a moment, but looked away quickly.

"I hope they do come to visit," he said, "but I don't think the situation is right for them to come live with me just now." He took a drink of his beer and frowned at it thoughtfully. "Although, if I wait too long, they'll be all grown up."

"And I don't want to get in the way of that," Janine said. "I think it's important for you to be there for your daughters, whatever it takes." Her expression turned wistful for just a moment. "But," she continued, turning back to him and reaching across the table to put her hand on the back of his, "I don't want to lose what we have here."

Victor thought about that for a moment. He tried very hard not to frown, and almost succeeded. "What is it that we have here?"

"I don't know," she said. "Possibilities?" she asked, trying the word. "Is that right?"

"Possibilities," Victor repeated. He nodded. "That sounds about right."

————

In the dream, Victor is on a mission with his team, and they're tasked with making contact with a target. It's nighttime, and they're moving through a densely populated residential area. The dream doesn't exactly match any mission Victor was ever on in real life, and nobody states what, precisely, they are to do when they reach the target.

But Victor knows this is a mission of violence.

The weather is fortuitous. It's raining hard, with thunder and lightning. The storm gives them a little cover, hiding their noise from people and especially from dogs. They are hurrying. They are soaked to the bone, and though the day is hot, the rain is cold. He feels the rain in his eyes and down the back of his neck.

They reach the target's home. Victor and another man climb onto the roof and take up positions to provide cover for the inside team.

Things begin to go wrong.

The light is blotchy, and kids are outside playing in the rain. In a flash of lightning, he can see them swinging something on a long string. The thunder rumbles quickly. The storm is close. Those kids shouldn't be out in the lightning like this.

Victor and his teammate squat on the roof. The rain picks up. Rain runs down the roof in sheets, and he can feel it trickling inside his boots.

Another flash of lightning splits the night, and this time the thunder cracks within a second. The wind picks up, hammering the rain against his back and exposed neck. They shouldn't be up on this roof. Where the hell is the rest of the team?

Suddenly, another pair of kids joins the others in the yard. It's *his* daughters. What are they doing here? Did they follow him?

The other kids notice them. The tone of their voices turns from joyful to harsh, and they go to confront his daughters. One of them pulls out a knife.

"Hey!" Victor shouts. Breaking the silence is a breach of protocol, but he has no option.

One of the kids looks at him, points, and opens his mouth to shout.

The kid with the knife doesn't keep going for his daughters.

But now, his oldest daughter doesn't look like herself anymore. She looks like the young woman in the bar.

Victor has no choice. He's in a cold panic, and he raises his rifle to his shoulder and aims it at the kid with the knife.

And, in a way that seems odd to him, although the dream *feels* real, and it catches his breath and quickens his pulse, Victor realizes that it is not real, even amid the terror of it.

Though the horror always feels fresh, he's grown used to it.

After all, with some variations, he's had the same dream at least once a week for a decade.

————

Angelina did not answer her phone any of the times Victor called on Thursday. When he called Friday evening, however, she picked up on the first ring. "I'm sorry," she said. "I've been busy, and I didn't want to take the time to fight with you."

"I didn't call to *fight*," he said. "I just want to know what's going on, and I have a right to talk to my daughters, you know. You can't keep them from me."

"I'm not—" Angelina started to say, then she cut herself off, and Victor heard her take a deep breath. "I don't want to fight with you, Victor," she said, "but I need to move on."

"Move on?" Victor asked.

"You knew Larry moved in with us."

"So you're marrying Larry now?"

"No—I don't know. We haven't talked about it, but—" she said. "*We* need to get things right between *us*."

Victor waved his hand as though she could see him. "I thought they were."

"No, we've been in limbo for almost three years," Angelina said.

"It's not three. It's two years and—"

"It's time, Victor," Angelina said. "And not just for me, or for you, for our girls, too."

Victor felt as though he should say something, but he could think of nothing.

"They need to know what's going on in their lives, too," Angelina said.

"They're still my daughters," Victor said. "I don't care how long you're with Larry. He'd not adopting them."

"He's not asking that, and—It's *way* too early to even think about that kind of thing, but I would never agree to that," Angelina said. "When the girls' friends ask them about their parents, though, I just don't want them to have to say, 'I don't know.'"

"And it would be better for them to say 'divorced'?" Victor asked.

"Yes," Angelina said quietly. "I'm sorry."

———

Happily, despite the terrible call with his wife, Victor did get to talk to his daughters. They filled him in on what was going on at school and at the "weird" church Larry had started taking them to. Thinking of Mills, Victor wasn't happy to hear about the church, but it was probably harmless enough.

But if he ever found out it wasn't, he would intervene. About other people's children, he could have moral ambiguity and hesitate. With his own daughters, he would not hesitate. Probably *could* not.

These thoughts, of course, led his mind back to Melissa, the young woman at the poker bar with Jordan, the moron. Where were her parents? Could it be possible that her parents were separated, her mother overworked and her father out of state, possibly even in North Carolina?

Sure, it was possible.

And if the roles were reversed, and someone else was in a position to make a difference for his daughter—

He was spinning his wheels again. He knew that going over the same old stuff in his mind again wouldn't make him feel any better, but he did know something that might.

It was Thursday night, still before eight. With the bus on the weeknight schedule, he could be there soon after the game started. He didn't know what he might do when he got there.

But as he put on his shoes and his coat, he was excited to find out.

CHAPTER NINE

As the bus rumbled across the Mississippi River and on into East St. Louis, Victor realized that this was similar to the missions he'd been on in the Special Forces, in that, while they usually had a sketch of a plan before they embarked on a mission, they inevitably found that reality was different from what they expected. Frequently, even the original objective had to be scuttled in favor of something else. Eventually, it got so that he knew that every mission was going to be improvised from the time they left until the time they got back.

The uncertainty gave them a boost of adrenaline, and after a while, he felt like he was hooked on it. More than that, knowing that he could *always* come up with a solution to *any* problem, on the fly, under pressure, made him feel ... invincible.

Well, invincible except for the team members who died along the way, and the certain knowledge that, sooner or later, it would be his price to pay.

The adrenaline boost sure was intense, though.

It was twenty minutes past eight when Victor got off the bus at the same stop as before. This night wasn't as cold as

Sunday had been, and Victor lit a cigarette as he walked to the bar. A few more people sat on the patio outside tonight, some of them not even huddled around the electric space heaters.

Once again, Victor stopped on the patio outside and looked in through the window at the dining room. A few of the faces were different, and most of them were in different places, but it was more or less the same game. And as before, Melissa sat in a chair behind Jordan.

Remembering that he'd been spotted last time he was here, Victor sat at one of the outside tables where he could see in through the window without being obvious. A few minutes later a waitress came out—a different one tonight, perhaps Janine's age with blond hair pulled back in a braided ponytail— and Victor ordered a bottle of beer.

While he waited for the beer, he considered what to do. When he was in the Special Forces, on a mission, he could find something—maybe not the *best* solution, but certainly *a* solution—on demand, every time. It reminded him of what he'd heard an artist say before, that when he got out the canvas and the paints, the muse showed up, every time. And she brought gifts. It had been like that in the Special Forces.

Here, though, tonight, he had nothing. Where was she?

The waitress came back in a minute with the bottle of beer, and Victor gave her cash. He opened the beer, lit another cigarette, and turned his attention back to the game. The waitress went back inside, and a minute or so later she reappeared in the dining room. She said something to one of the players, and he stood up and said something to her. He turned back to the table, put his hands on his hips, and stared at the cards and chips, slowly shaking his head. A moment later, he turned away and headed back up the dining room, toward the window where Victor was watching outside.

Victor frowned, turned his head away slightly, and

scratched his forehead to obscure his face. The player didn't notice him, but as he got close, Victor recognized the man as the player he'd seen from the bus the other night, the one with the yellow knit cap. He wasn't wearing it tonight, but his hair was standing, unruly as though he'd been wearing the cap all day.

The man turned, walked through the archway, and disappeared back into the main part of the bar out of sight.

Victor frowned, wondering where the man was going. There were bathrooms at the back part of the dining room, so that wasn't it. He wasn't looking for the waitress, because she had just talked to him. Could she have told him he had a call at the bar? Did people even still do that?

The front door swung open, and the player from the bus stepped out, pulling his yellow hat on as he did. He carried a fresh glass of beer in one hand, and he was trying to get a cigarette out of a pack with the other. He made his way down toward the table where Victor was and, smiling, gave him a wave with the hand holding the beer. "Are you going to play today?" the man asked. "Or are you just watching?"

"I think I have to just watch today," Victor said, feigning modesty. "I got here too late to play."

"You can get into the game for the first hour," the man said. "They let people in until the rebuys stop after the first hour." Without asking, as if he and Victor were old friends, he sat down at the table with Victor, positioned so that he could watch the game through the window as Victor had. After setting his beer down on the table, he was able to get a cigarette out of the pack and light it. "I'm probably going to rebuy, too," he said to Victor. "I just want to have a cigarette and cool off for a bit before I go back in."

The man proceeded to tell Victor a bad-beat story, and Victor pretended to listen. As he did, however, he continued to watch the action inside—and it got more interesting. Jordan seemed to say something rude to one of the other players, and when the guy said something back to him, he waved a hand to dismiss him and gestured at the back door. The message, as Victor understood it, was either for the other player to leave, or to fight him outside.

Yellow hat man noticed the action as well, and he chuckled. "That Jordan's a fun guy," he said, "but he's been too juiced up lately."

"Juiced up?" Victor asked.

"Yeah," the yellow-hat man said. "You know what I mean."

Victor did not, but everything it *might* have meant was bad.

"And TJ is not having it tonight," the yellow-hat man said.

"TJ?" Victor repeated.

"Yeah, the big guy," yellow-hat main said.

Victor said nothing, watching and waiting.

"TJ's big, but Jordan'll fight him if it comes to that," the yellow-hat man said, sounding amused.

"Oh, yeah?" Victor said.

Yellow hat man scoffed. "Jordan's been in three fights in the back alley since last year," he said, and added with a laugh, "that I know of."

"Wow," Victor said.

"I know. He's fearless," the yellow-hat man said. He shook his head and blew smoke at the window. "But one of these days he's going to mess with the wrong guy."

———

Victor and the guy with the yellow hat finished their cigarettes, then Victor stayed outside while the young man went back inside the Rusty Crown. Victor watched through the window as the tournament director made some announcement to the players. He still had no idea what he was going to do, but he felt as though an idea was coming.

A moment later the yellow-hat man reentered the dining room. He went to the tournament director, who saw him coming, and handed him a pair of paper bills. The tournament director took the cash, counted it, and handed him a short stack of poker chips, and the man put them down on the table in front of the seat he'd been sitting. It looked to Victor like he was back in the game.

As the players finished the hand they were playing, most of them stood up from the table. Victor realized it must be eight o'clock—time for the break. As they had done previously, the pudgy guy with the baseball cap, the large man named TJ, and a few of the other players went out the side door.

Jordan finished the hand and stood up, still looking at the cards on the table but reaching for a pack of cigarettes in his pocket. Melissa stood up, too. Finally, the action on the table completed. Jordan moved toward the side door, but suddenly turned to the yellow-hat man. His expression changed from interest to scowl, and he looked at the dining window at the front of the room again. If he could see outside, he could see Victor.

Though he wasn't sneaking or trying to hide, Victor still felt a thrill as though he'd been caught. He wondered what would happen next.

The answer came quickly. Jordan, looking angry, put a cigarette in his mouth, handed the pack to Melissa, who looked confused, and marched right up the dining room toward Victor. At the front of the room, with the cigarette hanging from his lip, he peered out the window at Victor. Apparently, he couldn't see very well, but he could see all right, because a look of recognition came onto his face, and he looked—unreasonably—angry. Then he turned toward the bar to the left and marched through the archway into the bar.

In the background, Victor saw the tournament director looking in Jordan's direction, shaking his head in disappointment or disgust. With his hands still full of chips, he went through a doorway at the back of the room to what looked like a service area.

A moment later, the front door flew open and Jordan came out, followed slowly by Melissa. He turned to his left, spotted Victor, and came over toward him. "What are you doing here?" he demanded. He put his hands on his hips and seemed as though he might actually be flexing his muscles to try to impress or intimidate Victor.

Victor, feeling neither threatened nor particularly offended, didn't get up from his seat. As Jordan stood facing him, Victor sized the man up. He had a rather square jaw and a thick head. He was medium height, and the muscles of his arms and legs looked larger than normal, but to Victor they seemed more swollen than developed. To Victor, he looked like someone who was using steroids together with weight training, but who was using the former more and more and the latter less and less. Overall, he seemed not inconsequential, but not generally imposing. At least, not to Victor.

Victor was keeping his right hand free, holding both his cigarette and his beer in his left hand, and he waggled them at Jordan. "Having a drink and a smoke," he said. Then, because he found Jordan generally distasteful and wanted to annoy him, he added, "What's it look like?"

Jordan wanted to run with it. "It looks like you're here trying to talk to my girl again," he said.

Victor put his beer on the table and took a drag off his cigarette. "Would that bother you?"

Jordan had lit his own cigarette, and as he jammed the

lighter back into his jeans pocket, he blew the smoke at Victor. "Last guy that did that got busted up."

Victor tipped his head with a small grin. "You know she's young enough to be my daughter, right?"

Jordan smirked.

Victor took the grin off his face. "She's almost young enough to be yours, too."

"Well, I already have a daughter," Jordan said, indignant. "What's your point?"

"My point is that I'm just having a drink and a smoke," Victor said. He waved the hand with the cigarette, making a little swirl of smoke. "And I'm thinking about playing some poker."

Jordan scoffed at him. "Do whatever you want, asshole," he said. "Just stop looking at my girl."

With that, turned and marched back into the bar, shepherding Melissa along in front of him. Victor rolled his eyes and shook his head behind Jordan as he stormed away, then turned to watch again through the dining room window.

A moment later, Jordan and Melissa appeared going through the archway into the dining room. The waitress with the braided ponytail followed after them, giving them stern looks and gesturing at them at the side door, and Victor guessed she was complaining about the lit cigarette Jordan was carrying. Jordan said something back to her, but he kept walking to the side door, and he and Melissa went outside. The waitress waved her hand in front of her face as though to clear the smoke, then turned and went back into the bar area.

The tournament director had returned, and he was changing some of the chips out on the tables. At that moment, Victor felt a strong urge to go to him and get into the game. He had no doubt that doing so would set Jordan off, and that would be fun. However, he remembered that he wasn't here because of Jordan, he was here because of Melissa, and he couldn't see how that could help.

More than ever, though, he wanted to do something to get Melissa away from Jordan.

That guy was trouble.

CHAPTER TEN

Friday morning, Victor called Lou again. "Are you still on stakeout?" he asked.

"Yeah," Lou said in disgust. "It's small-time stuff, but we're still on it."

"Cool," Victor said. "You need anyone to watch the place while you're in the can?"

"It couldn't hurt," Lou said. "I spend a lot of time in the can after lunch."

"Yeah, well, I've heard too many steaks will do that to you," Victor said with a grin.

Victor got ready and caught the bus, and a little before noon he walked into the little diner and found his friend sitting in the same booth as before. "Aren't you worried about being noticed here all the time?" Victor said with a frown as he sat down. "Or that the staff might rat you out?"

Lou looked at the diner and scoffed. "It's no worse than sitting in a car for getting noticed," he said. "And the local police give this place plenty of business. If the staff here ratted us out, they'd lose all that." He focused a frown in the direction of the waitress and a cook visible through a window in the kitchen area. "Plus, they'd be accessories to felonies."

"Felonies?" Victor said. "Things are that serious?"

"You bet they are," Lou said. "The St. Louis Police Department does not waste the taxpayers' money on petty crimes."

"But you still enforce misdemeanor laws, right?" Victor asked.

Lou shook his head at the suggestion. "Do you want the free lunch or not?"

Victor up his hands in a no-offense gesture and grinned. "I'm here, aren't I?"

The waitress came around, and they ordered lunches. Victor had the same as before, a burger and fries, and Lou, perhaps heeding Victor's word on the steaks, had the same. While they waited for their food, Lou complained about the chop shop across the street, which seemed to be a genuine thing, just small scale. Lou was watching it now to see if seemed to have connections to organized crime, and so far he was coming up short. "Watching a boring bunch of wannabes," was how he put it.

Victor listened politely to his friend, and when Lou seemed to have reached a natural pause in his complaining, he slid in a casual question: "Do you happen to have any connections over in East St. Louis?"

Lou shook his head in disgust. "Come on, Victor," he said. "Tell me you haven't been across the river looking for trouble."

"Not looking for *trouble*," Victor said, "looking for *poker*." He told Lou how he had gone over to the poker bar, almost making things up as he went along. "I thought if I became part of the game, I might have some fun." He paused a moment and picked up a French fry. "And maybe also be in a position to influence people to make good choices."

Lou was shaking his head, not believing any of it.

"But what I found, I think," Victor said, "was a felony."

Lou rolled his eyes. "A felony?"

Victor nodded. "Steroids are still illegal, aren't they?" he asked. He told Lou about his encounter the previous night. "Thick head, inflated muscles, uncontrollable temper," Victor said. "Classic steroids."

"Maybe, Vic," Lou said, shaking his head again, "but nobody's going to go after a guy based on that." He wiped his mouth with his napkin. "Muscles, temper—that's almost *every* guy under thirty-five."

"Thick head, too," Victor said.

Lou scoffed. "If anybody in that bar's got a thick head, it's you."

Victor groaned. He had known that Lou going for this was a long shot, but he was disappointed anyway.

"Listen, Vic," Lou said, adopting a serious tone. "You need to stay out of East St. Louis. If you don't, I'm afraid you really will be mixed up in some felonies, but they won't involve steroids."

Victor lifted his burger and took a bite.

"Tell me you won't go back there—or anywhere else—looking for trouble," Lou said.

Victor shook his head and shrugged. "Okay, I won't go looking for trouble," he said. Then he added, under his breath, "Only poker."

"God damn it, Vic," Lou said.

———

Saturday evening, Janine called Victor. "Have you been researching the case?" she asked.

"Um, no," Victor said. Chandler had told them to keep looking into it, but he'd forgotten all about it. "Not yet."

"I've been here at the library looking into it for a couple of hours," she said. She made a noise like shuddering over the phone. "It's pretty bad. You want to meet me at Tango, and I can show you what I found?"

"Um," Victor said. It sounded much better than doing the research himself. "You don't mind me copying your home-work?" he asked with a grin.

"Not at all," Janine said. "I know how busy you are."

Victor chuckled to himself at the word *busy*. "Sure," he said. "I'll meet you there in a half hour."

When Victor stepped into Tango, he found Janine again at the same table where Chandler had been. She looked up when he entered, and he gave her a wave, then ordered a beer and sat down with her. She had a bunch of papers spread out on the table in front of her, and she was studying one in her hand.

"That's a lot," Victor said, waving his non-beer hand at the array of papers.

"You're telling me," Janine said. She seemed to catch herself, and she looked up at him with a bright smile. "Hi, stranger," she said. "I haven't seen you in a while. How've you been?"

Victor smiled. "I've been ..." He felt his smile wane and his forehead crease as he thought about the past several days. It seemed suddenly that he always had a beer in his hand. "... busy," he said.

"Me, too," she said, apparently not noticing his expression or hesitation.

"So," Victor said, pulling out a chair and sitting down at the table with her, "Trever Mills is a bad guy?"

"Oh, yeah," she said. She looked among the papers on the table, shifting some of them around, until she found a copy of what looked like a newspaper article. "His great-grandfather

Horace Mills was a revival preacher in a tent in the dust bowl days in Oklahoma."

"That's going back a ways," Victor said.

"I know, right?" Janine said, looking up at him. Her eyes were alight with intrigue. "This was a long time coming." She looked down at the papers and shifted them around again. "Anyway, during the dust bowl he moved the family to Texas, and his son—Trever's grandfather—built a church in the swamps and turned it into a snake ministry."

"Snakes?" Victor said, genuinely surprised. "Didn't see that coming."

"I know, right?" Janine said. "He built a one-room church down in the swamps by Trinity River and ..." She shook her head in amazement. "People came for that. I mean, it was enough to make a living."

"Wow," Victor said. "But that can't still be going on, can it?"

"No," Janine said, shaking her head and taking a drink of her beer. "He died in eighty-five." She pawed through the papers on the table, found another one, and held it up with a smile. "Snakebite."

"Wow," Victor said sarcastically. "Didn't see that coming."

"I know, right?" Janine said. "So Trever's father took over, but he had bigger plans than snakes."

"It was the eighties," Victor said with a grin. "Who didn't?"

———

Sunday, Victor caught up on the grocery and laundry errands and spent some time looking through the condo, considering how he might arrange and rearrange things to make the place comfortable for himself without at the same time feeling like he was erasing the memory of his parents. It was a somber, lonely task. He spent most of the time walking from room to room with memories washing over him, and the only thing that seemed right for him to do was to continue staying in the guest bedroom and not change anything.

As the sun began to set, Victor began to feel restless. He took a beer and a cigarette out onto the balcony, sat in the chair, and watched the color drain from the sky and the lights of East St. Louis come on.

He was coming inside for another beer when the phone rang. He let it ring until he had the beer, then answered it.

"Hey, Vic," Lou said. "What are you up to tonight?"

Victor looked at the beer in his hand. "Pre-gaming, I think," he said.

"Pre-gaming?" Lou asked.

"Yeah," Victor said. "It's where you have some drinks before you go out somewhere, so you can get drunk without having to pay the price at the—"

"I know what pre-gaming is," Lou said. "You and I did it in London, and Prague, and even Dublin that one time."

"London and Prague, yes," Victor said. "But in Dublin we were pretty much just drinking that whole weekend, and I'm not sure that really counts as—"

"It counts, damn it," Lou said.

Victor laughed and stepped back out onto the balcony. Instead of sitting down, however, he put his beer on the table, lit a cigarette, and leaned against the railing.

"I meant," Lou continued, "where are you going that you need to be pre-gaming?" He paused. "Tell me it's not East St. Louis."

"It's not—I mean, it's not like that," Victor said.

Lou groaned in frustration.

"I just feel like playing some poker," Victor said. "Is that so bad?"

"God damn it, Victor," Lou said. He lowered his voice. "Not tonight, all right?"

Victor sensed something in his friend's tone. "What are you talking about? Why not tonight?"

"I—I called a friend on the East St. Louis P.D.," Lou said. "I told him I got a tip about a steroid dealer at that bar."

Victor took a drag off the cigarette, intrigued, but not convinced. "Really?" he asked.

"Yeah," he said. "I told him what you said—I may have embellished it a bit—and he was interested. He's going to go down there undercover tonight and play in the game, and if it looks like you said, he's going to try to make a buy from your friend."

"Jordan," Victor said. "Did you tell him his name?"

"Of course I did," Lou said. "I gave him everything you told me."

"Wow," Victor said. "I did not see that coming."

"Now, he asked me not to tell you at all, because it's an undercover operation and all that, but I had to call you anyway, because I know you," Lou said.

"Meaning what?" Victor asked.

"Meaning I know you'll probably go down there unless I talk to you. Were you going to go down there tonight?" Lou asked.

"No," Victor said.

"Liar," Lou said. "You already told me you were thinking about playing poker tonight, remember?"

Victor shrugged. "Yeah, but I didn't say where."

"Huh," Lou said. "And dealing drugs is a felony, but you know what else is?"

"Lots of things, unless they've changed the—"

"Assault," Lou said. "So I can't let you go there not knowing there will be an undercover there and getting yourself arrested in Illinois for a felony—"

"And crossing state lines to commit it, too," Victor said.

"Yeah, crossing state lines," Lou said. "But I also can't have you going there with the undercover, because if he senses you know, he could call off the whole thing."

Victor was quiet at that.

"Understand, Victor?" Lou said. "My friend is going there tonight, and if it all works out, your man Jordan is going to be arrested."

"I get it," Victor said.

"So can you please stay away from East St. Louis for one night?" Lou asked.

Victor stared out across the Mississippi at the lights of East St. Louis. He could see the bridge the bus crossed, and he thought he could see the road as it continued a few miles into the city. He felt like he could be helpful.

"What if something goes wrong?" Victor asked Lou. "What if your friend has trouble?"

"Then he'll call for backup," Lou said, "and the last thing they need is a vigilante in the way. Please tell me you're going to stay home."

Victor stared across the river, picked up his beer, and took a deep breath. "Fine," he said. "But if I get drunk at home and play the music too loud and the neighbors call the cops, it's your fault."

"You're a grown man, Vic," Lou said. "Keep your damn music down."

CHAPTER ELEVEN

On Monday, Victor called Lou several times, but Lou had no information about how the undercover operation had gone, or even whether it had happened at all. "Sorry, Vic," Lou said at the end of the day in frustration. "That's not how cops work. This is just a job. We don't have any personal care in most of the crimes, and if I call too much, he's going to wonder what's going on with me. I could even get written up, or they could even start to think I was in on it somehow and come after me."

This did not make Victor feel better, and he spent most of the day wondering how he might find out more. He didn't seem to have any options, though, at least not until the next game on Thursday.

Monday evening, Victor headed into class with his thoughts still on what might have happened at the poker bar. Or, it seemed more likely, what had not happened.

To his surprise, the class was abuzz even before Chandler took attendance and stood up. Everyone except Victor, it seemed, had done some research on Trever Mills.

Together, except for Victor, the class had dug a lot of sordid history on the Mills family and dirt on Trever Mills.

Janine had found the most information about the family's history, and even Chandler listened with rapt attention as she described the family's migration from the great-grandfather's tent revival church to the grandfather's one-room snake ministry. Everybody thought it was poetic justice that Trever's grandfather had died of a snake bite.

Even, surprisingly, Dapper Dan. He disagreed with the murmurs of disgust, however, when Janine described Trever's father's turn to televangelism.

"He looked at all the televangelists getting rich on TV, and he said, 'Why not me?'" Janine said.

"Why *not* him?" Dapper Dan asked. "You think Jesus wants people to be poor and unsuccessful?"

Trever's father had used his televangelism success to build a megachurch, and everybody had found amazing stories of the wealth his ministry generated. The Mills family amassed a fortune including mansions in Texas, Florida, and Caribbean islands, exotic cars and boats and recreational vehicles, a private jet plane, and so much more.

"A true embarrassment of riches," Chandler said.

The class adopted a more somber mood, though, as the talk turned to Trever Mills. One child made public accusations a year earlier, and a new District Attorney had opened an investigation.

And the more they looked, the more they found.

By now, dozens of people, all boys and young men, had come forward to say that Trever had molested them. And unless all of them were lying, Trever Mills had been molesting children at the summer camp from the time it opened—even molesting boys older than he was at the time.

"It's like he had some kind of sick aptitude for it," Jayson said.

"Remember," Chandler said as they discussed the case, "we're not trying to establish whether Trever Mills is guilty or innocent. We're merely looking at this case for the ethical questions it provides. Next time, we'll divide into our groups, and you can select a question and work on building arguments to support an answer to it." He took a deep breath and gave them a wary look. "So," he said, "be prepared."

———

Tuesday morning, Victor felt like he needed to go see Spence. He wasn't sure why, but things were weird, and he thought being in Spence's shop might give him an idea.

Spence had a shop downtown where he bought and sold guns. He bought and sold other interesting things, too, but the guns were where the money was, and they were the most consistently fun things to handle, so that was what he tended to talk about when people walked in the door.

"Good morning, Mr. Storm," Spence said when Victor walked in. He was a tall, thin man with dark skin, and he liked to wear a long, dark brown duster that Victor always suspected covered enough weapons to outfit a posse. "You look like a man who appreciates a reliable backup gun," Spence said.

A "backup gun" was a handgun to use in the event that your primary weapon had jammed or otherwise become unusable. They had to be rugged and reliable, because they spent most of their time tucked out of the way, and, by definition, they only got used in situations where other guns had already failed or been taken. Only once had Victor had the opportunity to fully appreciate a backup gun, but it had fully earned his gratitude. Lately, though, he was doing his best to solve his problems without a firearm of any kind. "I certainly do," Victor said, "but that isn't what I'm here for today."

"Well, my man," Spence said, "what *have* you come for today?"

Victor frowned. "I'm not exactly sure, Spence," he said. "I think right now I'm hoping your merchandise will give me an idea."

"Well, that's guaranteed," Spence said. "My merchandise never fails to give people all kinds of ideas." He chuckled. "And some of them are even good."

"Thanks," Victor said. For the next several minutes, he walked up and down the aisles of Spence's small shop. The guns in the shop were in either in the display case against the far wall or mounted to the wall above it. The shelves along the aisles did not have guns, but most of them were dedicated to gun accessories. Victor perused the cleaning kits, scopes, holsters, grips, stocks, and bullets of every caliber, all without much interest. Shelves on another aisle had non-firearm weapons like knives, crossbows, and even blow darts. A few other shelves along the window and the short aisle by the door had more generic accessories like targets, parachute cord, carrying bags, and first aid kits. It was this collection that drew Victor's interest.

The varied items reminded him of the mission kits his unit prepared before heading into hostile territory where they needed to leave nothing that could be traced back to his unit, or even the military. For such missions, each team member would assemble a kit consisting of nondescript, untraceable weapons (primary and backup), non-military and unmarked clothing and footgear, accessories such as rope from non-military sources, more cash than seemed reasonable, and identification that led not to a real person but to a dead end.

Suddenly, Victor was thinking of his excursions into East

St. Louis. Such a kit seemed to make sense for those adventures, for the same reasons as when he'd used the kits before.

Of course, thanks to his ingrained habits of staying prepared, he had most of the items to assemble such a kit already. Except one.

Victor wandered back over to the display case, where Spence was looking over a stack of paperwork. "I was wondering if you might have something, Spence," he said, "maybe somebody found it and turned it in to you."

Spence gave him a crooked smile. "That happens sometimes," he said. "What did you lose?"

"Not me," Victor said, returning Spence's smile. "It's a friend that kind of looks like me—about the same height and weight, you know."

"Yeah?" Spence asked. "What did he lose?"

"His identification card," Victor said. "He was walking down the street, and it must have just fallen out of his pocket."

"Ain't that the damnedest thing?" Spence said.

"It sure is," Victor said. "So now, my friend wants it back, and he's even offering a cash reward. So, if you *do* have it, I could give you the money for it, and he can pay me back later."

Spence was nodding. "You know, that *does* happen sometimes," he said with a smile. "Let me just lock this front door, and I'll see if I have your friend's identification in the back."

———

Victor arrived at class on Wednesday angry and frustrated. He'd called Lou as much as he could without pestering him, but he was unable to find out what had happened at the poker bar.

And he began to suspect that nothing had.

And, when he remembered that he was going to be

working with Dapper Dan in class, he wished he could skip it altogether. He gave serious thought to withdrawing from the class, but he didn't want to repeat what he'd done so far, and he also didn't want to quit the classes altogether, so working with Dapper Dan Turner seemed to be his only option.

In frustration, he thought about pre-gaming the class, but he wouldn't be able to function if he went drunk enough to enjoy it, and only a few would leave him too dull to work.

In class, they quickly divided into groups, and Victor found himself feeling sorry for Dapper Dan. Though he had always seemed outspoken and unwavering in his views, he seemed almost scared of Victor. Victor remembered what Chandler had said about being intimidating, and he thought maybe there was some truth to it.

Regardless, the work was dull. Victor had little interest in exploring the ethical questions of Trever Mills's case, and Dapper Dan seemed to have little ability to form an ethical question without quoting something from scripture. Making things worse, Victor could hear the other groups talking around him, and it seemed as though they were all having a better time than he was, and coming up with better questions.

In the end, the question he and Dapper Dan agreed to explore was: *If Trever Mills is guilty, but the legal system lets him go, would it be right for someone else to punish him?*

It was Victor's idea.

———

Thursday night, Victor took the bus across the river into East St. Louis. He knew that Lou would be pissed if he messed up the undercover operation, but he was only going to find out what was going on with it. If he saw it going on, he'd stay out of the way, and if wasn't going on—and it really seemed like it wasn't—there was nothing to mess up anyway. Either way, Lou would never know.

Easy, right?

He left a little before seven-thirty, planning to get to the Rusty Crown right when the game started. The winter weather had abated a little, and he wore a jacket instead of his heavy coat. Just in case of trouble, he also tucked a pair of black motorcycle gloves into the pocket. He did not, however, take a weapon. He was serious about playing in the game, and he didn't want to sit right next to the other people in the game with a concealed weapon on his person—particularly if one of them was a cop.

The bus rumbled across the Mississippi River into Illinois, stopping here and there to drop off or pick up passengers. Sometimes the motion of a bus made him drowsy, but tonight he felt amped up in anticipation of what he'd find at the poker bar.

Before long, however, the droning of the bus set his mind wandering, and he found himself thinking of Trever Mills. Dallas wasn't all that far from St. Louis, almost certainly no more than one day by bus. Maybe Victor could take a trip there and see the Trinity River Christian Outreach camp first-hand. In fact, if he wasn't mistaken, Trever Mills was out on bail. Maybe Victor could talk to him. Sometimes the wheels of justice got stuck in a rut. Maybe Victor could help them along.

It wouldn't be the first time.

Suddenly he was jolted out of his thoughts when he saw a familiar yellow hat come up the stairs at the front of the bus. The man flashed his pass to the driver, and Victor recognized him instantly. He was the yellow-hat man from the poker bar, of course. Victor was sitting in the back of the bus, in the front of the elevated section past the back door, and the man also spotted him at once. He gave Victor a wave like they were old friends, then came back and sat in the seat across the aisle from him.

"Where are you headed tonight?" the man asked with a smile.

"Same place you are, I think," Victor said.

"Oh, yeah?" the man asked, looking surprised and a little suspicious. "Gonna watch the game again?"

Victor feigned a chuckle. "Nah," he said. "I thought I might play in it tonight."

The man raised his eyebrows in surprise. "Oh, really?" he said. He cringed a little at the idea. "Jordan might not like that."

"No?" Victor asked. "Why's that?"

The man looked at him directly. "He thinks you want something with Melissa, after you tried to talk to her that one night."

Victor shrugged. "If she's happy with him," he said with a wry smile, "what does he have to worry about?"

"See, that right there," the man said. "Saying stuff like that is the kind of thing that makes him upset."

"Well," Victor said. He was happy that he'd bothered Jordan, and pleased that the man recognized that he was doing it on purpose. He shrugged again. "What's the problem if I just want to play poker?"

The man shook his head, looked forward up through the window, then turned back to Victor. "I don't think Jordan's going to like it."

Victor smiled. "We'll see."

CHAPTER TWELVE

They arrived at the stop a few minutes later. It was a few minutes after eight, and they hustled down the sidewalk to the Rusty Crown. Victor appraised the situation as they arrived. No one stood outside the side door, but a few more people than before sat on the front patio smoking, perhaps because of the warmer weather, and though a couple of them looked in their direction as Victor and the yellow-hat man approached, they seemed ordinary. Victor couldn't see the parking lot, which was on the other side of the building, but he wouldn't have expected to see anything unusual anyway. Victor let the other man lead as they got close to the bar, and he followed him as he opened the door and went into the bar.

Inside, they turned right and headed through the archway to the dining room. In the back, the poker game had already started. As previously, the players were seated at the two tables in the back of the dining room. Victor noted that the pudgy man was here again, as were Jordan and Melissa in their usual arrangement. There were a few faces that Victor didn't recognize, but they all looked vaguely familiar, and he hadn't been paying close enough attention to everyone before to be sure if any were new to him.

Victor looked around the rest of the bar. It looked like a slow night. Only a few patrons sat at the tall chairs at the long wooden bar, and only two or three of the tables in the main bar were occupied, and none at all were occupied in the dining room except for the ones with the poker players. No one in the bar seemed to be paying any attention to the poker players. If there was an undercover cop here, Victor thought, he must be in the game.

The tournament director saw them coming and gave them a big smile. He had been standing by the table on the left watching the action, but now he came back toward the supply table to get them chips. The other players turned to see who was coming several of them waved at the yellow-hat man, and a few gave Victor a friendly nod. Jordan started to smile at the yellow-hat man, but he did a double-take when he saw Victor, sitting up straighter and turning sideways in his chair.

The yellow-hat man took his hat off and stuffed it into his coat pocket as he walked to the back of the dining room.

"Hello, Darryl," the tournament director said to the yellow-hat man.

Oh, he has a name., Victor thought with a smile. *Darryl.*

Darryl took his chips, and the tournament director gestured for him to go to the table on the right.

As Victor stepped forward, the tournament director turned to him with a smile. "Going to play tonight?" he asked.

"Yep," Victor said. He tried to smile himself, but it felt weird, and he probably just looked constipated. "First time."

"Good, good. It's going to be a lot of fun," the tournament director said. He reached to hand Victor a stack of white, red, and green poker chips and turned to gesture at the table where Jordan was sitting. "You'll be at—"

"Oh, *hell* no," Jordan said, getting up. "Not this guy," he said to the tournament director.

The tournament director froze, the chips still in his hand, looking startled and a little nervous. He turned to Jordan. "What?" he asked.

"This guy's been bothering Melissa for a week," Jordan said. "No way he gets to play."

Victor felt surprised, too, and he felt his neck get warm. This was not a good way of staying unnoticed. "I'm just here to have some fun—" he started to say.

"Shut it, idiot," Jordan said to him. "How would you like it if I got on that bus and followed you home and bothered you at the Y or wherever the hell it is you stay, huh?"

Victor stopped talking and closed his mouth. Jordan knew he had come on the bus?

"Hey!" yelled someone from the bar area. Victor turned his head slightly and saw the surly barman had stood up and was shouting in their direction. "Don't mess up my dining room," he said. "If you've got a problem, take it outside!"

"There's no—" Victor started to say.

"Right, let's take it outside," Jordan said, turning toward the side door.

Frankly, Victor would have enjoyed thrashing Jordan outside, inside, or anywhere else he had in mind, but there was the small matter of the undercover cop here somewhere, and he was going to have a hard time getting a steroid connection from Jordan if Jordan was in the hospital.

Jordan had reached the side door, and he turned to yell back at Victor. "Are you coming, or what, powder puff?"

Victor looked around, hoping the undercover cop would put an end to this nonsense, but if he was here, he was staying undercover.

Then he spotted Melissa. She had stood up and moved

over by the wall close to the door. She was obviously trying to stay out of the way so she wouldn't get hurt, but Victor thought he saw something else as well. There was a gleam in her eye, a spark of excitement. She was fully on Jordan's side. She liked this.

But how would she feel about Jordan if she saw him handled easily?

Victor took a deep breath and walked to the door. Only one way to find out.

Outside, Jordan raised his arms into a fighting pose, arms wide for pummeling, hands open but relaxed, ready to open-slap or ball into a fist and punch as warranted. He had bulging neck muscles, and Victor was even more sure Jordan was using steroids.

Jordan had left his jacket inside. Victor still had his on, and he raised his hands in front of himself, making fists like an untrained amateur would, trying to make his body language appear weak and timid to draw Jordan in.

It worked. Almost immediately Jordan stepped forward and swung his right fist at Victor's head. Victor shifted his body sideways and back just enough to get out of the way.

Jordan recovered from the missed punch and threw another with his left hand. Victor ducked the other way to avoid that one as well.

Frustrated, Jordan threw five or six punches in a row, stepping forward and grunting with each one. Victor bobbed and weaved his head as he stepped backward, nimbly staying just out of Jordan's reach.

Jordan stopped his attack and straightened a bit to catch his breath.

"Already out of breath?" Victor said, taunting. "What kind of tough guy are you?"

"Come at me!" Jordan said.

Victor scoffed at him.

Jordan lunged at Victor, head down, arms wide.

Victor caught Jordan's forearm as he closed the distance, pushing it down and to the side. Off balance, Jordan swung his arms and tried to get hold of Victor, but missed as Victor slipped away.

Seething now, Jordan lunged again, and once more Victor evaded him, this time catching his other forearm and slipping away to the other side.

Jordan turned to Victor, panting, his face red with exertion and anger. "Come on, asshole!" he shouted.

Victor shook his head and laughed, mocking him.

Jordan let out a yell of rage and charged at Victor again.

This time, Victor feigned stepping away, but at the last moment, he turned to meet Jordan squarely. He caught Jordan's outreached forearm with his hand, but instead of pushing it down and to the side, he raised the arm and swung his forearm against Jordan's chest. At the same time, he planted his foot, shifted his weight, and stepped behind Jordan's leg.

Jordan's eyes went wide as he realized the helplessness of his position, but it was too late.

In a smooth move, Victor pushed Jordan backward. The moron couldn't step back to keep his balance, and he fell. Now gripping Jordan's shirt, Victor added his weight to Jordan's fall. Jordan landed flat on his back on the asphalt, and Victor's additional weight knocked the breath out of him. Victor let go of the moron and stood up, watching for Jordan to kick or flail at him in some way. The takedown had knocked the wind out of Jordan, however, and it was all he could do to gasp and struggle to catch his breath.

Victor looked at the crowd of poker players who had followed them out the side door. The shock on their faces told him they had never seen anyone handle Jordan like that before. The pudgy man took off his ball cap and scratched his bald head. Yellow-hat man Darryl looked back and forth between Victor and Jordan, his mouth open in unabashed surprise. Victor couldn't help but feel a little pride. It was always fun to give the smackdown to someone who truly deserved it.

What he did not see, however, was anyone acting like a police officer, undercover or otherwise.

"You assholes!" shouted a voice from the doorway. Victor turned and saw that it was the barman. He had come to the side door, and he stood with one hand against the frame and the other against the door's crash bar. "I've got paying customers in here that want to leave now because you assholes have to fight in the goddamn parking lot!"

"It's okay," the tournament director said, holding up his hands and looking from the barman to Victor and back. "It's all done."

"You're goddamn right it's all done!" the barman yelled. "The game is canceled!" With that, he turned and stormed back into the dining room, slamming the door behind him as he went.

The poker players groaned in complaint.

Victor looked down at Jordan, who was still flat on his back on the ground, then stepped away from him. Melissa, who had been up against the wall by the door, rushed over to Jordan. She reached down to help him up, but he slapped her hands away and rolled over to get up under his own power.

"Does he mean forever, or just for tonight?" Darryl asked the tournament director.

"Don't worry about it. I'm sure it's just for tonight," the tournament director said. He gave Victor a dirty look, then, in a louder voice, he turned and said to the players. "Sorry the game is canceled, everybody," he said. "I can't do anything about it tonight, but I'll talk to the owner, and we'll have the game again on Sunday."

Victor took one more quick look around. With the game broken up and no police in sight, there seemed nothing left for him to do. He turned and headed across the street to the bus stop.

CHAPTER THIRTEEN

The phone was ringing when Victor got back to the condo Thursday night. It was about nine in the evening, which was too late for most people to call. And after what had happened at the bar, Victor was worried that it could not mean anything good.

"Sorry I haven't been returning your calls," Lou said on the phone when Victor answered. "That chop shop case has turned out to be something bigger, and my guy in East St. Louis wasn't returning my calls anyway."

"Okay," Victor said. "No problem."

"Anyway," Lou said, "what he said was that he hasn't been able to get over there yet."

"He hasn't?" Victor asked in surprise. "It's been almost a week."

"Yeah, well, he's not in a rush," Lou said.

"Obviously," Victor said.

Lou groaned. "When I told him what you saw, he said it sounded like the smallest of small-time, and he's got plenty of big fish to catch as it is, but he would get there when he can because the information came from me."

"So, what does that mean?" Victor asked.

"It means don't get your hopes up," Lou said. "Besides, even if he got arrested, it wouldn't mean he would go away. He would take a plea and be back for the next game."

"Even if he took a plea," Victor said, "he wouldn't do time?"

Lou scoffed. "He's a white guy, right?"

"Yes."

"Then he's not going away for steroids," Lou said. "Unless they get him on assault or better, he'd be back for the next game."

"So, if he gets in a fight with me, that will put him away?" Victor asked.

Lou groaned. "Just a fight? Mutual combat? I don't think so." He chuckled. "Now, if you don't fight back, and you let him break some of the bones in your face ..."

"Wait, he wouldn't get put away for assaulting me, just because I fought back?"

"For a healthy dude like you, he's not going away for long unless he puts you in a coma," Lou said. "Now, if you were a cop, that'd be a whole different story."

Victor scoffed. "So, that's the function of our justice system?" he said. "To make the country safer for police?"

Lou let out a laugh that was more mocking than humorous. "Now you're getting it."

———

After he hung up with Lou, Victor wondered what this new information meant.

Probably, it meant that he was on his own again with the Melissa situation. He probably had been all along, but he just hadn't realized it.

He got a beer and a cigarette and went back out on the

balcony to stare over into East St. Louis and think. Amazing, he thought as he twisted off the top of the beer, then looked at his knuckles. He'd been in an actual fight, had left a guy embarrassed in front of his girl and gasping for breath on the ground, and he hadn't even bruised a knuckle. He didn't think he'd even thrown a punch. Amazing.

He took a drink from his beer, a drag off his cigarette, and stared out at the twinkling lights.

He realized that, after spending some time at the poker bar and seeing Melissa and Jordan more, she didn't remind him of his daughter as much. And after seeing her rush to help Jordan after he'd put him on the ground, he doubted he'd tarnished Jordan's image in her mind. Probably nothing he could do would make a difference with her at all. And even if it did, why was it any of his business in the first place?

Wouldn't his time be better spent worrying about his own daughter?

Yes, it would.

The problem was, he just *didn't like* Jordan. The guy was a jerk. Unfortunately, it didn't sound like Lou's friend was in a hurry to get over to check him out. Victor felt almost ready to let the whole thing go.

Still, he could go back to the bar a few times and see if anything came up. He wasn't going to let Jordan land a punch if he could help it, let alone break any of his bones, but he thought that if he was there, Jordan wouldn't be able to resist taking a swing at him. At a minimum, he'd like to see Jordan get arrested, even if he *did* get a cushy plea deal.

As long as he could avoid getting arrested himself.

———

Friday afternoon, Victor met Dapper Dan at the St. Louis Community College library to work on their group project. At least, he thought, it would take his mind off his other concerns for a while.

And it didn't hurt that Janine was going to be there, working on her group project with Loretta. In fact, most of the class had arranged to meet at the library to work on their group projects at the same time. Almost everyone except Chandler would be there.

They had planned to meet at the work desks upstairs, and Janine and Dapper Dan were already there when Victor arrived.

"Hi, stranger," Janine said. "Haven't seen you in a while."

"I know," Victor said with a smile. "It's been a couple of days."

She returned his smile. "Are you staying busy?"

He thought about his adventure at the poker bar. Though they had been seeing each other for a while, and she had seen him beaten up, he had never told her about what he did when he went looking for trouble. He shrugged. "Not the way I'd like," he said.

Loretta arrived soon after they went upstairs, and Victor's heart sank a little as she and Janine went off to sit together to work on their assignment, leaving him with Dapper Dan.

For what it was worth, Dapper Dan looked more disappointed to be working with him than the other way around. He was dressed in slacks, a pressed shirt, and a tie, as usual, and he carried himself with an air of business, but he avoided eye contact with Victor, and his body language suggested they'd be working the same area, but not precisely *together*.

"Okay," Victor said, taking a seat at the table where Dapper Dan was sitting with his notebook open in front of him, "what's our ethical question again?"

Dapper Dan looked at his notes. "'If Trever Mills is guilty, but the legal system lets him go, would it be right for someone else to punish him?'"

"Right," Victor said. Dapper Dan seemed a little uneasy around him, and Victor felt a little tinge of guilt. Dapper Dan wasn't a *bad* guy. Victor found his fixation on what was in the Bible a little annoying, but he wasn't doing it to *be* annoying. It was just who he was. "Any thoughts on that question?" Victor asked.

Dapper Dan shifted in his chair and glanced at Victor. "Mostly, I'm just happy that it's one of the easy ones."

"One of the easy ones?" Victor repeated.

"Yeah," Dapper Dan said, raising his eyebrows. "I mean, the answer is obviously 'yes.'"

"It is?" Victor asked.

"Of course," Dapper Dan said with a frown. "For a million reasons."

"Okay," Victor said, feeling a sense of relief. Victor had brought along a portfolio with a pad of paper and a pen in it, and he opened it on the table. "Let's write some down."

For the next several minutes, he and Dapper Dan talked over various ideas, looking for fundamental truths to build upon. Unsurprisingly, Dapper Dan had several ideas that came straight from the Old Testament, eye-for-an-eye and that sort of thing. To his surprise, Victor agreed with many of them. And it was easy to assemble them to support the answer to their ethical question.

Even more surprising, Dapper Dan seemed to relish the idea of making sure Trever Mills didn't go unpunished.

On this issue, at least, he and Dapper Dan seemed to be on the same wavelength.

When they had a list of reasons to punish Mills on the table, Victor sat back and narrowed his eyes at the list. "Okay," he said. "We've got plenty of reasons to punish Trever Mills no matter what." He nodded a little. "And they sound good to me."

"And to me," Dapper Dan said.

"But," Victor added. "What of these could we say are *fundamental* truths, *necessarily* true?"

"All of them," Dapper Dan said, frowning down at the list. "Most of them are in the Bible."

Victor cringed. "Just because something is in the Bible, that doesn't mean it's *necessarily* true."

"Even if you think that," Dapper Dan said, "it doesn't mean it's *necessarily* not true."

"Okay," Victor said, not wanting to argue. "Let's find some that *are* necessarily true."

They scanned the list together again, and it turned out to be easy to find things that *were* necessarily true, or at least *felt* so:

Don't kill other people.

Don't harm other people.

Fundamentally true.

"Okay," Victor said again, frowning at the list now, "but how do we get from there to the idea that it's acceptable to harm someone who has done these things?"

Dapper Dan was frowning at the list, too. "If that's what it takes to stop someone from harming other people?"

"Right," Victor said, testing the idea in his head. "So it would be okay to harm that person, to make him stop harming other people."

"If it took harming him to make him stop harming other people," Dapper Dan said, "then you could describe that as *necessary*."

"Necessary," Victor said, "to harm that person."

"If that's what it took," Dapper Dan said.

"Or even to kill him?" Victor asked. "If that's what it took?"

Dapper Dan looked down at the list, then back up at Victor. "I guess so."

Victor nodded. "Let's write it down."

While they were each putting down the argument on the page, Janine came back over to their table, Loretta right behind her. "Loretta found something," she said. "There's news about the case."

Seeing her excitement, Victor sat up in his seat. "What is it?" he asked. "Did more victims come forward? Did he confess?"

Janine shook her head. "An anonymous source from the District Attorney's office spoke out," she said. "Apparently they're close to a plea."

"A plea?" he said. Suddenly, Victor's conversation with Lou rushed back to him, and a chill ran through him. "So, he'll be going away for a long time?"

Janine looked shaken. "I hope so," she said.

Dapper Dan said, "Shit."

———

"So, how was your time with Dan?" Janine asked him.

Victor raised his eyebrows and tipped his beer like a salute. "Actually, not too bad," he said. "Much better than I would have ever expected."

"Really?" Janine asked, in genuine surprise. "I thought he got on your nerves."

"He always has in class," Victor said, "but when we were talking together, we kind of thought alike. It was weird."

"Well, that's good, then," Janine said.

After the library meeting, Victor and Janine had gone to Tango for a quick drink. That was three drinks ago.

"How was your time with Loretta?" Victor asked.

"A little bit maddening," Janine said. "She was fixated on the legal case, and every time I tried to pinpoint a truth we could start from, she would veer back to 'those poor babies.'"

"What is your ethical question?" Victor asked.

"'Should Trever's father be partly to blame for what he's done, since he made him a counselor at the camp and kept him there even when kids started complaining?'" Janine said, pointing her beer at the air as if remembering reading it off a blackboard.

"Ah, the old parent question," Victor said.

"Yep," Janine said.

"And how's it going?" Victor asked.

Janine shook her head. "So far, we have 'those poor babies' and 'that man ought to be ashamed of himself.'"

Victor nodded. "Yes," he said, raising his beer in a toast. "Eternal truths."

Janine laughed, then turned to Victor with a serious look in her eye. "Do you have any plans for this weekend?"

"I don't know about the rest of the weekend," Victor said, "but Friday afternoon I'm going to have drinks with my girl-friend, then maybe we'll get some dinner, and ... who knows—" He cut himself off abruptly.

Janine was staring at him in shock.

He thought back on his words. Fuck. He'd said *girlfriend*.

"Well," Janine said with a sly smile. "That's sounds fun."

CHAPTER FOURTEEN

Saturday morning, Victor woke up at five o'clock, as usual, in Janine's bed, which was less unusual every time. He sat up in bed, but did not get up. For a while, he just watched her sleep, thinking about everything. It seemed, despite both his best and worst intentions, that they were, after all, in a relationship.

He'd even referred to her as his girlfriend.

When he'd said it, it had been a shock. Although they'd been spending more and more time together, and he'd been waking up more often in her bed, he'd denied it to himself. In fact, he'd been thinking it was *important* to deny it. For her safety.

He was, after all, still having the dreams. He hadn't had one this past night, at least not that he remembered, but he remembered having one the previous time. Sometimes, the dreams gripped him as if they were real and made him sit up in bed, made him flail out—

Made him dangerous.

It wasn't just the dreams that had made Angelina leave, but they were part of it. He remembered when he was in basic training for the army decades earlier, and an old-timer in one of the bars had warned him: "Think about what you do over there," he'd said, "because you bring it back here with you." Victor and his friends had dismissed him at the time. But it turned out he was right.

But maybe, just maybe, he thought, Janine was different. After all, his experience had made him a different man from the one Angelina had married, changed him into a monster. Janine had never known him before. She had only known the monster. And she liked him.

Of course, she didn't really *know* the monster, not completely, anyway. She had seen him bloody, and she knew he was finding trouble, but she didn't know he was *looking* for it. She probably suspected, but it was probably worse than she thought.

He was probably worse than she thought.

How could he not be?

This line of thinking, he realized, was unhelpful at best. He was in a funk, and he needed to get out of it.

He reached over in the bed and traced his fingertips down Janine's naked back.

At his touch, she wriggled and inhaled deeply, and with a smile, she rolled onto her side, cocked one leg up under the sheet, and stretched the other. Her eyes opened and blinked a few times, and she looked up at him.

"Hey, there," he said. "Are you awake?"

She rolled her shoulders and looked at him. He was not dressed yet, and she seemed to register this fact. "Not yet," she said, closing her eyes again and adjusting her pillow. "I'm still sleepy." She opened one eye and looked at him again. "What are you doing?"

"Just thinking," he said.

She groaned. "You woke me up for just thinking?"

He stroked her back with his fingertips. "I thought maybe we could get some breakfast."

She moaned and shifted under his fingers, her moves becoming more sensual. "Right now?"

"Maybe not quite yet," he said. "Maybe we should stay in bed a little longer."

———

It was still morning, but barely, when Victor's bus rolled up to the stop near the condominium tower where he lived. His night and morning with Janine had left him feeling upbeat, optimistic even, and the world seemed brighter. He was—unusually for him—in a really good mood.

That changed abruptly when he saw a man with a familiar yellow hat sitting on the bench under the shelter at the stop. As the bus approached, the man didn't get up, instead looking at the driver and shaking his head, a gesture that meant there was no need to stop for him; he wasn't getting on. But he was standing up. He was waiting for someone.

Victor's attention snapped to a focus.

As the bus rolled to a stop, Victor recognized the man. It was indeed Darryl, the man from the poker bar with the yellow hat. And there was no doubt who he was looking for.

Victor had stood up as the bus approached the stop. Usually, he got off the bus via the back door, and, obviously anticipating this, the man's attention was on the back door. Instead, Victor lowered his body slightly and walked quickly to the front of the bus. Victor had pulled the cord to signal the driver for a stop, but the driver had not seen him come forward, and no one was waiting to get onto the bus, so when the bus was stopped, the driver opened the back door and looked up in the mirror, frowned at seeing no one getting off.

"Front door, please," Victor said.

The driver opened the door, and Victor stepped off the bus onto the sidewalk. He hit the ground in a sprint, not away from Darryl, but right at him.

Darryl had been watching the back door for someone to get off, and, like the bus driver, he was a little confused as to why no one did. He'd apparently heard the front door open, though, and he was just turning toward it when Victor got to him.

In another part of the city, or in another city, Victor was polite and gentle until he couldn't be anymore. When trouble followed him home practically to his doorstep, however, it should expect him to meet it with violence.

Victor grabbed Darryl's collar with both hands and shoved him up against the metal wall of the bus stop shelter. The move was as aggressive as he dared to be with a bus full of witnesses right next to him.

"What the fuck?" Darryl spluttered, trying to keep his balance as Victor kept pushing him off it.

Victor heard the doors of the bus hiss shut, and the engine rumbled louder as the driver drove it away.

"Hey, hey!" Darryl said as he recognized Victor. "It's me, Darryl, from poker."

Victor kept him pressed against the wall of the shelter with a firm grip on his collar. "I know who you are," Victor said. "What the fuck are you doing here?"

"I came to see you, all right?" Darryl said.

"I *know* that," Victor said through clenched teeth. "Why?"

"Jesus," Darryl said, struggling against Victor's grip. "I'll tell you. Just let me go."

Victor looked around them quickly. The day was cold, and few people were outside walking around. He saw no one who seemed interested in either Darryl or himself. He turned back to Darryl, let go of his collar, and took a step back from him.

Darryl huffed and straightened his coat as he got his feet back under himself. "Jesus Christ, I came here to do you a favor, dude," he said. "I came here to warn you."

"*You're* warning *me?*" Victor said, still full of intensity.

"It's not *me*, dude," Darryl said. "It's Jordan."

Victor's eyes narrowed at the name. Again he looked back over his shoulder, and again he saw no one threatening. He turned back to Darryl, gripped the lapel of his coat in one fist, and pulled him out onto the sidewalk. "Come on," he said, walking down the street away from his the condo building. "This way."

Darryl stumbled but stayed on his feet, and he hustled to keep up with the quick pace Victor was setting.

After they'd gone fifty yards or so down the sidewalk, Victor again looked over his shoulder. They seemed to be alone.

"How did you find me?" Victor demanded of Darryl. "And where is Jordan?"

"I don't know where he is right now," Darryl said, "but he's looking for you."

"Why?"

"You really have to ask?" Darryl said. "He was super embarrassed when you kicked his ass in the alley." He scoffed and shook his head. "In front of his girlfriend and everybody."

"Good," Victor said.

"No, not good, dude," Darryl said. "When you left that night, he made Melissa drive us, and they followed the bus when you left." Darryl paused to let this sink in.

Victor gave Darryl a dark look. "How did he know I was on the bus?"

Darryl raised his eyebrows. "I guess I mentioned it to

him," he said, "but it's not like you were hiding. You went to the stop right across the street."

Victor thought about this for a moment. He'd been careless. Of course, he couldn't have known Jordan even existed when he first went there. But he was looking for trouble, after all. "He made Melissa drive?" Victor said.

"Yeah," Darryl said. "His license got suspended after his last DUI, so he's afraid to drive."

"I see," Victor said.

"It's her car, anyway," Darryl said. "Her father bought it for her."

"Of course," Victor said, shaking his head. He gave Darryl a shrewd look. "And you were with them. I suppose he *made* you go, too."

Darryl shrugged. "He's my friend."

Victor felt his forehead crease in concern. Of course, it had always been possible for anyone to follow him when he took the bus, at least more or less. He never imagined that anyone would be so determined as to actually do it.

"Of course," Victor said again in disgust. He took a deep breath. "So if you know where I live, why were you looking for me out here on the street?"

"Man, we don't know *exactly* where you live," Darryl said. "I mean, we saw you get off the bus at this stop and start walking, but Melissa couldn't get the car turned in time, and we lost you." He paused a beat. "I thought Melissa did it on purpose."

"Good," Victor said. He looked at Darryl. He seemed flustered, but sincere. "I appreciate the warning," he said.

Darryl shrugged. "I like Jordan, but he gets out of control sometimes." He shook his head. "I don't want him to get into trouble again."

"No," Victor said dryly, "we wouldn't want that."

"Good," Darryl said. "So, you'll stay away from poker, then?"

"Oh, hell, no," Victor said. He stopped walking and looked Darryl in the eye. "You tell Jordan I'll be there Tuesday night."

———

"Tuesday night?" Lou said on the phone. "Didn't you say they play on Sundays?"

"They do," Victor said. "The thing is, though, I'd rather not have a rematch with that idiot. There's nothing in it for me."

"But you told his friend you'd be there on Tuesday anyway," Lou said.

"Well, I don't want him coming around here looking for me," Victor said. "I don't want him knowing where I live." He shook his head. "I had to tell him someplace else."

"So you think if you embarrass him again on Tuesday he'll leave you alone?" Lou asked, his left eyebrow raised slightly. "Because that's not the way things happen."

"Of course not," Victor said. "Can't you call your East St. Louis friend and tell him to nab Jordan before Tuesday?"

Lou laughed mirthlessly. "That's not how it works, Vic," he said. "For one thing, we don't even know for sure that this Jordan guy is doing anything illegal."

"Bah," Victor said.

"And for another thing," Lou said, "he already said he doesn't think this is major, and he's got bigger fish to fry."

Victor scoffed. He knew Lou was right, and he didn't see a way out of this trouble.

"This kind of thing is going to happen when you go looking for trouble," Lou said. "That's why I keep begging you to knock that shit off and go to the VA?"

Victor took a deep breath and said nothing.

"Listen," Lou said, "I'll call my friend, but I don't think he's going to get to anything before Tuesday night. In the meantime, just lay low in your place for a while. That Jordan guy will lose interest after a few days."

Victor sneered. "*Hide* here in this condo? From that asshole?" he said. "I can't do that."

"Of course not," Lou said in disgust. "What are you going to do then?"

"Well, I plan on being here tomorrow, and Monday evening I have class," Victor said, "but Tuesday I'm going to play poker at the Rusty Crown."

"Of course you are," Lou said. "Of course."

CHAPTER FIFTEEN

Late Sunday afternoon, Victor was taking a nap in the guest bedroom at the condo when the phone rang and it was Angelina calling.

"Did you get the papers filled out?" she asked.

"No," he said, still groggy, "I haven't had time yet."

"Haven't had time?" she repeated. "It's been two weeks. What have you been doing? Did you finally get a job?"

"What? No," Victor said, disappointed in himself because she was right, but angry because she was attacking him. "I've had ... you know ... class and stuff."

"Victor," she said, using his name as an epithet.

"Anyway," he said, "what's the rush?"

"It's not a rush, Victor," she said. "I just want this to be over with."

Victor thought he heard a tone in her voice, a note of disdain, and suddenly he felt that she was in a hurry to get him out of her life, eager to leave him behind, and that irritated him. "Don't worry," he said. "I'll get it done, and before you know it, you'll have forgotten all about me."

Angelina made a sound on the phone that sounded like a sob. "It's not that, Victor."

Victor scoffed. "It's okay, I understand," he said. "You've got a new man now, and you want to cut things off with the last one."

"No—" Angelina said.

"I'm still going to be around, you know," Victor said. "I *am* still the girls' father."

"Victor, it's not—"

"And I'm always going to *be* their father, which means that you're going to be stuck having me around for as long as—well, until death do we part, I guess, which is rather ironic, now that I think about it."

"It's not that, Victor—"

"It's okay," Victor said, interrupting again. "Like I said, I can handle it."

She hung up the phone then, but before she did, he could hear that she was crying.

And he was not happy with himself.

With a burning sensation in his chest, he went to the middle of the living room and stood in the gathering darkness. His hands felt jittery, and his breath was shallow.

What he wanted more than anything was to go to the Rusty Crown and get into a fight. He knew, however, that if he did, he would have a hard time restraining himself.

The last thing he needed was for a fight to become a murder. If Darryl could track him down, the police almost surely could.

So he kept his feet planted while he thought. All he needed, he realized, was something to distract him until it was too late to make the trip.

Beginning to cool down, he realized he hadn't had dinner yet. That's what he would do. Something with brown rice that would have to cook for forty minutes. It would be too late then.

Afterward, he supposed, he might look at the divorce papers, at least give them a read-through.

Or maybe he would go straight to bed.

———

In the dream, he's carrying his service rifle, and he's trying to keep the stock hidden. He's surrounded by members of his former Special Forces team. They're not on a mission; they're just doing something around their headquarters. In the dream, it doesn't seem that there's a reason for them to have their rifles at the time, but it's a dream, and Victor has his.

And he's trying not to let the others see it.

Some soldiers carve a notch into the stock of their rifles for every confirmed kill they have in combat. Victor is one of those soldiers. Most of the men in his unit are. It's a way of remembering how serious what they are doing is.

Victor's unit has seen action. Virtually none of their stocks have no notches. Many have only one. Some have a few. A few have more.

Victor's stock is covered in notches.

He's trying to keep his covered with a rag used for shining boots, but it's too small.

And at the same time, he's carving another notch.

The rag keeps slipping as he carves furiously, and he feels terrified about being exposed.

"Whoa, there," says a voice. "What's that?"

Victor looks, and it's his first commander.

The commander looks closer, and Victor can smell the man's aftershave. "Why are there so many notches?" he asks Victor.

Victor shakes his head. "I can't stop," he says. He stops shaking his head and gives the man a steely gaze. The world goes quiet around him. "I don't want to."

———

Monday evening, Victor arrived at his class early. Despite what he'd told Lou on the phone, he was trying to lie low until Tuesday. If Jordan was looking for him, he didn't want to find him, and he certainly didn't want to lead him to Janine's place.

"Hey, stranger," Janine said to him with a smile when he walked in. "Are you ready for Spring Break next week?"

"I sure am," Victor said.

"Are you going to get crazy somewhere?" she asked playfully.

Victor smiled. "I just might."

Dapper Dan also arrived early. "I'm sorry," he said to Victor, "but we need to talk about our presentation."

"Presentation?" Victor said. Shit! He'd forgotten all about it. "Is that tonight?"

Dapper Dan shook his head. "Ours is Wednesday. We should meet tomorrow and go over it."

"Tomorrow's Tuesday," Victor said with a grimace. He shook his head. "I can't do that. I've got plans I can't miss."

"Plans?" Janine said, surprised. "What kind?"

"It's something—" Victor started to say, struggling. "I told my friend Lou I'd do something."

Janine made a face. "What kind of thing?"

Victor shook his head. "There's some undercover stuff I'm kind of involved in."

"Wow," Janine said. "Sounds exciting."

Victor shrugged.

"Well, our presentation is on Wednesday," Dapper Dan said. "Can we maybe meet early in the day tomorrow?"

"I'm sorry," Victor said. "But, like you said, ours is one of the easy ones. Do you think you can take the lead on this? I'll be up there with you, and whatever you want to say, I'll support it, but ..." He shrugged and shook his head again.

Dapper Dan sighed in obvious disappointment. "Okay, I guess," he said, "but it's supposed to be a *group* project."

"I know," Victor said, "and we *did* develop the arguments together, right?"

"I guess so," Dapper Dan said.

"Okay, then," Victor said. "Thank you for this, and I'm sorry, really."

Chandler came in then, and everybody took their seats. He wanted to start the presentations right after attendance. "Because I never know how long these things are going to take," he said.

Janine and Loretta went first, and Chandler had been right. The presentation should have been straightforward, and it probably would have been if Janine had been giving it by herself. However, Loretta kept interjecting statements about more accusations against Trever Mills, then treating the accusations as convictions he should be punished for. Victor kept waiting for Chandler to intervene and get the presentation back on track, but he didn't.

Part of the problem was the new material Loretta had found. Not only were there new accusations, but old ones had resurfaced as well.

"They knew about him seven years ago when he was sixteen and that boy Kolby French went missing," Loretta said.

Victor straightened at this, frowning. This was news to him. Given the murmur in the class, it was new to most of them. "What?" Victor asked.

"Everybody said he was the last one to see Kolby, but his father got him a lawyer and hid him away and nobody was ever able to find out what happened," Loretta said, visibly upset and almost on the verge of tears.

"It was Trever?" someone asked.

"Yes," Loretta said.

Janine shrugged. "It looks like probably," she said. "Kolby disappeared from the summer camp while Trever was a counselor there."

"And Trever went missing at the same time," Loretta said.

"Trever turned up after a few days," Janine said. "He said he'd had a 'religious experience' in the swamp, and he didn't know what happened to Kolby." She shook her head. "They never found him."

"The family hired a big lawyer, just like this time," Loretta said. "The father said he wouldn't be a counselor again, but he was back the next year, maybe the same year."

"That boy was only eight years old," Janine said. "He would be fifteen now."

"Getting his license, learning to drive," Loretta said. "Instead, he's gone, and that character is still running free."

The class fell silent. Even Chandler sat slumped in the chair at the desk at the front of the room, looking lost in thought. "What about the parents of the other kids?" Chandler asked. "Why did they continue to send their kids there?"

No one had an answer to that for a while. Janine, apparently realizing that their presentation had gone off the rails, looked at the paper she'd been referring to in her hand, then shook her head and lowered it. "That's it, I guess," she said, turning to Chandler. "I mean, we got sidetracked, but we said everything we planned on saying."

"Okay," Chandler said. He sat up in his chair and looked at the class. "Does anyone have any questions?"

Janine and Loretta paused and looked out at the class. No one had any questions, though, so they headed back to their seats.

"All right," Chandler said. "Next up, we'll have—"

"They have to," Dapper Dan said, interrupting Chandler quietly.

Chandler stopped and looked at him. "Excuse me?" he asked. "They have to *what?*"

"The parents," Dapper Dan said. "You asked why the parents keep sending their kids to the summer camp. The answer is, they have to."

"Why do they *have* to?" Chandler asked.

"Because God will protect the children, and God is in the church," Dapper Dan said. "If they don't trust the church, it means they don't trust God."

"They could *leave* the church," Jayson said quietly. "That's what I would do."

"You'd be leaving God," Dapper Dan said. "God works through the church, so leaving the church means leaving God." He looked down at his desk for a moment, then nodded. "At least, that's what they say."

The room fell silent as everyone considered this for a moment.

"Well," Chandler said, getting to his feet, "that sounds like it will lead to more ethical questions for our next project."

Two more pairs presented their projects, and Victor was happy that they stayed on track and went quickly and fairly smoothly. When they were done, it was already time to go.

"Okay, good job, everyone," Chandler said. "We've had a lot to think about tonight. Next time, we'll finish up our presentations and talk about what we'll do after Spring Break." He started to turn away, then turned back. "Oh, and if the news today was correct, perhaps Trever Mills's case will have been resolved by Wednesday."

"What?" Victor said in surprise.

Judging from the gasps in the classroom, everyone else seemed as shocked as he was.

Chandler raised an eyebrow at them. "I heard some news on the radio on my way here tonight," he said. "There's no official word, yet, but sources are saying that Trever's attorney may be close to securing a plea deal for him."

"For him to go away for a long time?" Janine asked.

"Well, I don't know, of course," Chandler said, "but I would think not. From what I've seen, the harsher the sentence, the longer it takes to get a plea to it."

"Here we go again," Loretta said in disgust.

"So you think that's what it will be?" Victor asked. "A slap on the wrist?"

"Well, like I said, I don't know," Chandler said, "but I hope not."

CHAPTER SIXTEEN

Tuesday morning, Victor woke up at his usual time and slipped out of bed without waking Janine. Trying to be quiet, he took a shower and dressed, but Janine woke anyway, and when he opened the door, she was waiting for him. She had put a robe on and made coffee, and she was sitting on the chair with a mug in her hands. She had left the light on in the kitchen, and the light was still on in the bathroom, but here in the bedroom, the light was dim.

"I poured you a cup," she said, gesturing at a cup on the dressing table outside the bathroom door.

"Thank you," Victor said. Feeling awkward, he picked up the mug. It was too hot to drink, but he sipped at it anyway.

She was studying him with dark eyes. "You don't have to leave, you know," she said.

"I ... do have to leave," he said.

"Not really," she said. "Not ever."

"It's not that," he said. "It's not ... you—"

She scoffed. "Is this the 'it's not you, it's me' speech?"

"No," he said. "Well, not exactly, anyway."

She was shaking her head. "What does that mean?"

"It means …" he said. He didn't know exactly what he was trying to say, and it wasn't going well. "I told you before: I'm dangerous."

She dismissed this with a shake of her head. "I know, you have weird stuff about you. Guess what? So does everybody!"

"It's not like that," he said. He took a deep breath. "You don't really know me that well."

"I don't know you?" she asked. "We've been friends for months, and more than that for a few weeks. I think I know you pretty well."

"Not like that," he said. He chose some words carefully. "There are people who want to hurt me," he said.

She looked at him as though trying to guess if he was serious. "What?"

He raised a hand. "It's okay," he said. "At least, it's going to be. It's just—it happens sometimes, and I don't want anyone to ever think they could hurt me … by hurting you."

She tipped her head forward and raised an eyebrow. "Are you some kind of criminal?"

"No," he said. "Well, maybe *technically* sometimes. But usually, the people who want to hurt me are angry because I stood up for someone else."

She let this concept register in her brain. "So, you're a *good* guy?"

"I wouldn't say that, exactly," he said. He thought for a moment. "Maybe."

"These people who want to hurt you, are they bad guys?" she asked.

"Yes," he said. "Always."

"Then you're a good guy," she said. Her brow furrowed, and a little smile crept onto the corner of her mouth. Then she turned to him, smile gone, but still frowning. "Wait, are you for real?"

He raised his eyebrows, surprised at the question. "Yes," he said. "I mean, that's the way *I* see it, though I'm sure opinions vary."

She looked lost in thought, considering the implications of what he'd told her. She stood up and paced across to the door of the bedroom, took a drink of her coffee, and turned back to him. "Is this where you go when you go out at night?"

He looked at her. He had told her way too much already. "Yes."

She chuckled. "I thought you had another girlfriend."

He chuckled, too. "No, I already have all I can handle," he said.

She sipped her coffee again. "Is that where you're going today?" she asked. "To deal with a bad guy?"

"Tonight, yes," he said.

"So, we can spend the day together?" she asked.

"A little while," he said. "Then I have to go home and get ready."

She nodded thoughtfully, and a mischievous smile came onto her face. "Can I go with you?"

He scoffed, but then thought about it. "No," he said. "Not this time."

———

In the afternoon, Victor took the bus and headed home. Janine had wanted to drive him, but he was genuinely concerned about what Jordan might do, and he wanted to keep her out of it. Now, he wasn't riding the bus straight home. Instead, he was taking the long way to come down a different route from the one where Darryl had found him.

But, more than just being evasive, he was using the trip to figure out what the hell to do.

Telling Janine the little he had told her felt ... awesome. Thrilling and exciting and sensuous even, but ... *terrifying*. He couldn't remember the last time he had felt comfortable enough with a woman to let her know this about himself. It was incredible. It felt amazing.

And it had changed everything.

He felt ... *potential* with her. Yes, *potential*. Instead of brooding by himself, he could ... he didn't know. Brood with her?

Maybe.

At any rate, he sensed that he had reached a point where he needed either to let her in closer to himself or to let her go. And until this morning, he thought he was on track for the latter option.

Maybe that was why he had started to tell her what he had about looking for trouble. He had thought it likely that she would be repulsed by that ... by *him*. But she wasn't. She was *intrigued*. Damn if she didn't seem as excited about this turn of events as he was.

So what did that mean? He still couldn't let her in on anything, obviously. She had no training in combat or covert operations, and she would be more of a liability than an asset if he was in a fight.

But, maybe he could talk to her before a fight, when he was trying to figure out the right thing to do, or afterward, when he was wondering whether he truly was a good guy or a bad guy.

He frowned. He'd have to figure out some way of doing that without making her an accessory, or not do it at all.

There was a lot to figure out, but it felt good to have someone to talk to. Even if he couldn't exactly *talk* about *every- thing* yet. At least she knew who he was, kind of, more than anyone else, anyway.

And she liked him.

But, keeping her close instead of cutting her free changed one other thing as well. He could live with looking over his own shoulder, but he couldn't be looking over hers. He had to remove that threat.

Somehow.

He did have an idea. It wasn't pretty, but it just might work.

————

When Victor got home, he called Lou right away, and he was happy that Lou answered.

"How's everything going?" Lou asked him. "Staying out of East St. Louis?"

"Yes," Victor said. "Well, lately. For the past several days, anyway. But it doesn't matter, I guess. I'm going over there tonight."

"What?" Lou said. "I can't help you with that, you know."

"I know—" Victor started.

"Actually, I can," Lou said. "I can tell you not to do that, and that will help you out because apparently you are not smart enough to know that on your own, so I'll tell you now: Do not go to East St. Louis. Do not go looking for trouble there. Or anywhere else, for that matter—"

"That's just it, Lou," Victor said. "I'm not going there looking for trouble. I ... I'm going there to ... make up with him, I guess."

"You're kidding," Lou said. "After throwing a hissy fit over every two-bit hood for the last six months, Victor Storm is going to kiss and make up with a punk."

"Well, that's not it, *exactly*," Victor said. "But that's the general idea."

Lou scoffed. "You care to tell me why?"

Victor took a deep breath. "Well, I don't want him coming after me looking for revenge, and I'm not going to kill him for looking like he's on steroids and his girlfriend being too good for him, so what other choice do I have?"

"None I can see," Lou said. "Which is why I said don't get mixed up in shit like that from the start."

"Well, I should have listened to you," Victor said. "This time, anyway."

Lou scoffed again.

"So," Victor said, "Can you call your cop friend and tell him to stand down?" Victor asked.

"Stand down?" Lou asked.

"Right," Victor said. "If I'm there and a cop shows up, he's going to suspect I had something to do with it—which I did—and like you said, he's almost certainly not going to do any time, even if he gets arrested at all." He took another breath. "So, if you could call your friend—"

"What?" Lou said. "No, I can't—You know that isn't how the police business works, right? Cops aren't like some kind of private security you can rent and send them here and there whenever you want and send them home when you're done."

"I know that, Lou—"

"I'm not sure you do, Vic," Lou said. "I'm remembering the last several times you've called me, and it seems like that's exactly what you had in mind."

"Come on, Lou. That's not fair," Victor said. "Is it too much to ask a cop to look into some illegal activity? And is it too much to ask a cop—who hasn't looked into some illegal activity because he thinks it isn't big enough for him—to forget about a report? Is that really too much? Is that what you're telling me?"

Lou scoffed. "I'm just saying that that's not how cops

work," he said. "We're not some kind of servants out there ... serving the public."

"Really?" Victor asked. "Protect and serve? That isn't you?"

Lou groaned. "Don't start with that protect and serve crap. We have jobs to do, and there are procedures for reporting crime, and we investigate those crimes, but we are not at the beck and call of everybody who thinks he saw somebody whose head's too big."

"I get it, Lou," Victor said. "Really, I do. And I should have listened to you from the start—"

"*This* time, right?" Lou said sarcastically.

"Well, yes, but lots of times," Victor said. "You've been a really good friend, and I should listen to you more."

"Like when I tell you to get your ass to the VA," Lou said.

"Well, yeah, maybe," Victor said. "One step at a time."

"One step at a time," Lou repeated.

Victor was quiet for a moment, almost biting his lip. Lou seemed to be calmed down, at least a bit. "So," Victor said hesitantly, "can you call him?"

"God damn it, Vic," Lou said. "Fine. I'll call him." He snorted. "But don't get your hopes up."

———

Tuesday evening, Victor took the bus across the river into East St. Louis. The night was colder than it had been lately, but he wore his medium-weight jacket instead of his heavy coat anyway. He wasn't sure what he was walking into, and he wanted to be ready for anything.

He watched the city lights scroll past outside the bus, and the farther he got into East St. Louis, the more doubts he had about his plan.

Probably because it was a terrible plan.

Tell Jordan he wanted to be friends now, or at least not to be enemies? What? After Victor had embarrassed him in front of his girlfriend last week? Jordan had been pissed enough to commandeer a car and follow Victor home as step one of a plan of revenge. Was he seriously going to let all that go just because Victor asked him nicely to? Certainly not.

And, to be clear, Victor was *not* planning on apologizing. Somehow, he intended to let Jordan know that he didn't want him to continue to be offended, *and yet*, he was not at all sorry for what had happened. Yeah, good luck with that.

And still, apologizing was not something that Victor could do here. He was *not* sorry he had interfered, and he realized that, when he got the opportunity again, he was going to *continue* to try to convince Melissa that she should not even hang out with Jordan, and certainly not be in a relationship with him. Victor wanted peace here, but he would *not* sacrifice his principles for it. Not now, not ever.

So, what was his plan, then?

He had no idea. It seemed likely that he was walking into another fight. He was probably going to kick Jordan's ass again, and probably worse than before. Was that going to make things better? No, it wasn't.

But what choice did he have? Sure, he could go back across the river and just lie low and hope that the whole thing blew over, but how would he know if it ever did? He could take the risk for himself, but he could *not* leave this loose end alone when it had the potential to harm people he cared about.

The bus rumbled on, ever closer to the poker bar.

Victor realized that he had no choice but to leave it to the muse. He would show up, and she would bring a solution. Just like his operations in the Special Forces. Just like jazz. He would trust the muse. It was the only choice he had.

And though it was a little scary, the muse had always shown up in the past. She would now, too.

Somehow.

This is what he was thinking when the bus rolled to a stop and he saw a yellow hat waiting to get on.

CHAPTER SEVENTEEN

"I don't know, man," Darryl said. His eyes had gone round, and he had a stupid little smile on his face. "Jordan's really pissed. I don't think he's going to accept your apology."

"No, no," Victor said, tipping his head and narrowing his eyes. "I'm not *apologizing*. I just want to tell Jordan that I want everything to be cool between us. I don't want to fight with him anymore."

"I don't know, man," Darryl said again. "If you don't want to fight, I'm pretty sure that's just going to make him want to fight *more*."

Victor scoffed. Darryl's description of Jordan was making *Victor* want to fight Jordan more. "Well, we have to try it," Victor said. "Will you talk to him?"

"*Me?*" Jordan said. "No. I want to stay out of it."

"Just talk to him and tell him I told you I don't want to fight," Victor said. "That's not hard, is it?"

Darryl made a face and shook his head. "I don't want him to think I've been talking to you," he said.

"But we're riding in on the same bus together," Victor said. "*Of course* we were talking."

Darryl was still shaking his head. "I don't know, man," he said.

Victor sighed. The stop for the bar was next. The bus driver was already coasting to a stop. "You said before that he was your friend and you don't want him to do something stupid, right?"

"Yeah, but that doesn't mean—"

"Just talk to him, then," Victor said. "We're almost to the bar. Just go in before me and say you saw me on the bus and I said I don't want us to fight. That's simple. Okay?"

Darryl was still shaking his head, his yellow hat flopping back and forth sideways. "Fine," he said. "I'll talk to him."

———

Victor lit a cigarette as they approached the bar, and when they got there, he let Darryl go into the bar ahead of him as he stood on the patio and watched through the dining-room window. The bus must have been a little earlier than last time, because the poker players were still getting chips from the tournament director and taking their seats. Several of them were still getting up from a table near the middle of the dining room, leaving behind an assortment of empty glasses and bottles.

Jordan was there, with Melissa standing beside him. He got a stack of chips from the tournament director and headed to a seat at the table on the right-hand side, and once again he sat in a chair with his back to the rest of the dining room, and Melissa sat at a table behind him.

Darryl came through the archway on the left into the dining room, taking his hat off and scratching his scruffy hair as he walked in. He seemed to sense that Victor was watching through the dining-room window, and he glanced at the window and gave a discreet wave before heading down the center aisle to get a stack of chips from the tournament director.

Darryl took the stack of chips in one hand, and Victor saw the tournament director point him to the table on the left, and he was happy to see that, instead of going there directly, Darryl first went over to Jordan. There, he bumped fists with Jordan, then said something to him.

When he turned and gestured at the window, Victor guessed that he was doing as he'd asked.

Victor put his cigarette out in the ashtray on the table by the window, then headed into the bar, wondering if Darryl's being on the bus had been the muse at work. Maybe, he thought. The muse did work in mysterious ways.

As he stepped through the front door and into the bar, Victor noticed that the bar was busier than he'd seen it before. The gray-haired barman stood behind the bar, leaning against the polished wooden top with a bar towel over his shoulder, talking to one of the patrons. A few other patrons occupied tall chairs pulled up to the bar, several of the tables had people sitting at them, and Victor even saw two young men playing pool at a table on the left side of the bar. He only noticed this out of his training and habit, however. His real interest was in the dining room.

As he walked through the archway into the dining room, Victor noticed that Jordan had gotten to his feet, and he was turning to come this way. Behind him, Darryl put a hand on his arm as if to try to hold him back, but Jordan shook Darryl's hand off and came up the aisle at Victor.

Victor, with a tepid smile and still hoping for the best, walked more slowly to meet Jordan in the center of the dining room.

"So," Jordan said as he drew near, "Darryl says you want to apologize."

Victor gave Darryl a disappointed look, and Darryl shrugged with a sheepish grin. So much for the muse. He looked back at Jordan, who was already so fired up that the veins on his neck were bulging. In fact, the muscles of his neck, shoulders, and arms all looked bigger. Good grief, Victor thought, had Jordan stepped up his steroid use and workouts for a rematch with him? He looked Jordan in the eye and tipped his head. "Darryl seems like a decent guy, but he's wrong about that," Victor said. "I only wanted a truce so that we can all play poker here and have some fun." He looked past Jordan at the tournament director and the other players as he said it, holding his arms apart in a gesture looking for acceptance.

The tournament director, holding a stack of chips in his hand, waited for Victor, his eyebrows raised hopefully. The pudgy man with the ball cap had pivoted in his seat so he could see whatever took place between Jordan and Victor, but he was tapping his chips on the table, ready to get started. The other players, seeming to recognize Jordan's volatility, had also turned to see what would happen.

Jordan broke into a creepy smile at Victor. "You just want to play? That's all?" he asked.

Victor nodded, trying to make a sincere smile. "That's right."

"Okay, okay," Jordan said, looking back and forth from the players to Victor. "Go ahead and apologize, and we can start the game."

Victor looked back at the poker players. They seemed to think that was a good idea. He looked at Jordan again, still smiling. "Apologize?" he asked. "For what?"

"For hitting me with that cheap shot in the parking lot,"

Jordan said, his smile turning intense, "and for hitting on my girl."

"Cheap shot?" Victor said. "*Hitting* on your girl?" He tried not to let his smile turn into a smirk, but he could feel that he failed at it. He looked at Jordan squarely. "Look, Jordan, we don't have to be friends, but can't we just play poker without all this ... drama?"

"Drama?" Jordan said. He stopped smiling. "Sure," he said. "Just apologize."

Victor shook his head slowly. "I can't do that, Jordan."

"Fine," Jordan said. "Then get the fuck out."

"What?" Victor said.

"You heard me, motherfucker," Jordan said. "Get the fuck out." He raised his hands and straight-arm shoved Victor hard in the chest.

Victor took a step backward, but kept his balance. "Come on, Jordan," he said. "This is dumb. Let's just play poker."

Jordan bristled at Victor's words. "Are you calling me dumb?"

He pushed Victor in the chest again, and Victor let him, but he turned his upper body to deflect the blow, keeping his own balance while using Jordan's attack to take his away.

The way Victor was able to knock him off balance without raising a finger made Jordan even angrier.

"Aw, come on, Jordan," said a voice behind Jordan. Victor didn't take his eyes off Jordan, but he recognized the voice as Darryl. "Just sit down so we can play."

"He's right," the tournament director said. "The clock is running. We need to get cards in the air."

Jordan pushed at Victor again, and again Victor turned to deflect the blow and let Jordan fall off balance. "Listen to them, Jordan," Victor said. "Everybody's just here to have fun."

"You want to play?" Jordan shouted at Victor, almost in a full rage. "Apologize!"

"You idiots!" the barman shouted from behind the bar. "You fight in my bar and I'm calling the cops!"

"Come on, Jordan," the pudgy man said. "Sit down. Let's play."

"Jordan, just come back and play poker," Melissa shouted at him. "Why do you have to ruin everything?"

At her words, Jordan spun to face her. "Shut your mouth, you little bitch!" he shouted, spittle flying. "You don't tell me what to do!"

"You know what, Jordan?" Victor said quietly. "I think I will apologize after all."

Jordan turned back to him. "All right, asshole," he said with a sneer. "Let's hear it."

Victor gave Jordan a hard look in his eye, then turned to Melissa with a softer expression. "I'm sorry, Melissa," he said. "This idiot is a first-rate loser, and I wanted to, but I couldn't find any way to get you apart from him, and for that failure, I apologize from the bottom of my heart."

Jordan's face had gotten redder and redder through Victor's "apology," and now he erupted in rage. He pushed at Victor again, and again Victor turned his upper body and shifted his weight so that Jordan succeeded only in throwing himself off balance. This time, though, he stumbled up against the table where the players had left their empty bottles and glasses. One of the bottles tipped over, rolled off the edge of the table, and broke when it hit the concrete floor.

Jordan, already bent against the table, spotted the broken bottle on the floor. Victor kicked at it, but he was too far away, and before he could get to it, Jordan had seized hold of the neck of the bottle.

He came up facing Victor with the bottle in his right hand,

and before Victor could find something for defense Jordan stepped forward, slashing at him with the razor edge of the broken glass.

Someone behind Jordan screamed, but Victor's attention was now too focused for him to know who it was.

Jordan stepped at him and slashed again. Victor backed up to stay out of range, but he bumped into the table that was up against the front wall of the dining room and could retreat no further.

Jordan slashed again. Victor raised his left arm to block the blow, and he felt a thump on his forearm as the edge of the bottle struck him and sliced through his jacket.

Suddenly there was a flash of movement behind Jordan, and somebody grabbed his arm from behind.

Jordan spun to face this new attacker, and Victor saw it was the man who had been at the bar talking to the barman.

"Freeze, asshole!" the man shouted. "You're under arrest."

Holy shit! Victor thought. *The undercover cop!*

Jordan did not freeze, and the cop retreated, trying to get something—probably a gun—out of the waistband of his pants. Before he could, however, Jordan lunged at him, swinging the bottle at the cop's face.

However, the distraction of the cop gave Victor all the advantage he needed. As Jordan stepped toward the cop, Victor kicked Jordan's back foot hard, sideways behind his other leg. Jordan couldn't stop his lunge, but he couldn't get his legs untangled in time to stay on his feet. He went down hard.

Before Jordan could move, the cop had jumped onto his back and was pulling his arms around behind him. Victor held Jordan's feet until the cop got the handcuffs on him, then stood up and stepped back.

The poker players had scattered as the pushing had turned into a fight. Some of them had retreated to the back door, evidently fearful of what Jordan could do full of rage with a broken beer bottle. Melissa, Darryl, and a couple of others had stood up and moved to the side of the room, apparently ready to let Hurricane Jordan blow itself out. Only the pudgy man still sat at the poker table, and he still held his chips in his hand, looking around and waiting for the game to start. Victor almost chuckled at the sight of him.

Victor went through the archway and sat at a table by the front wall, where he could see and hear what was happening but go unnoticed.

The cop hauled Jordan to his feet. Jordan seemed to struggle to recognize his situation, alternating between glaring at Victor and staring wild-eyed at the undercover cop as though wondering what was going on. All the while, he flexed against the handcuffs, and the muscles of his arms looked weak against the steel. The cop read Jordan his rights, then called for a police unit to come pick him up. When the cop made the call, Victor heard the terms *assaulting an officer* and *assault with a deadly weapon*, and he knew his work was finished.

Without waiting to talk to the cop or Darryl or Melissa or anybody, Victor slipped out the door and headed back to the bus stop.

As he walked away, he broke into a smile. The muse had come, and she had brought him a gift.

Like she always did.

CHAPTER EIGHTEEN

Victor arrived at class Wednesday evening still feeling the rush of what had happened Tuesday night. He still couldn't believe how well everything had worked out. He would call Lou to see if he could find out the official rundown on Jordan, but he was going to wait a while to let him cool down after their terrible conversation the previous day. He thought, however, that everything had worked out the best he could have expected. The last he had seen of Melissa, she had been heading out the side door with Darryl. He supposed that, if Jordan really *had* been involved with the illegal steroid trade, one or both of them might have been accessories somehow. They would have to resolve those problems on their own, however. He had done what he had set out to do, and he was feeling ebullient.

The mood in his class, however, seemed quite the opposite. The other students seemed down. Half of them were doing presentations tonight, and the other half were watching presentations, and neither of those activities was particularly fun for most people, but there seemed to be something else amiss that Victor did not know about.

Even Chandler seemed downbeat. Sure, his task this

evening was to watch people struggling to work through the most basic building blocks of ethics, and that could probably be classified as torture when applied to someone with Chandler's depth of experience, but still—Victor had a sense that there was something more going on.

The first two presentations went pretty smoothly. The groups had obviously benefited from seeing the work of the others on Monday, because they had copied the simplest and most direct approach. With his mind still racing about how he would describe the events of the previous night to Lou, Victor did not pay proper attention to the groups that went before him, but it seemed that their work was competent, if unremarkable.

Then it was time for Victor and Dapper Dan to give their presentation. They went to the front of the room and stood by the desk where Chandler sat, and Dan—Victor was in such a good mood that he was considering calling Dan by his proper name—started reading off the paper he'd brought. Victor stood by Dan with a smile, and he tried hard to keep smiling as Dan read their ethical question, launched into a list of Biblical citations that only seemed more-or-less related to it, then concluded with a statement that logic applied to universally accepted truths had been shown to answer their question in the affirmative.

The class was quiet. Chandler regarded them for a moment. This was the part where Chandler had been asking people if they had any questions about the presentations, but this time he was sitting in stony silence.

Victor took a deep breath and tried to look happy. "So, does anyone have any questions?" he asked, eager for the episode to be done, but also terrified that anyone would ask him about Dan's work.

Fortunately, none of the students had a question.

"I have a few questions," Chandler said.

Victor and Dan turned to him.

"Did you both work on this as a group project?" he asked.

"Yes," Victor said. "Of course."

Dapper Dan nodded.

"And, you're satisfied with the content presented here tonight, Victor?" Chandler asked.

Victor swallowed hard. "Sure," he said. He looked at Dan with a smile. "I think we nailed it."

"Very well," Chandler said.

With a sigh of relief, Victor headed back to his seat. He was sure the grade wasn't going to be good, but he wasn't taking this class for grades, anyway.

"All right," Chandler said to the class. "Good job on the presentations, everyone." There was a shuffle of activity as the students started to gather their things to get ready to go. "Next week is Spring Break, and I'm sure that when we get back the following Monday, we'll have much to discuss regarding Trever Mills's plea deal today."

"What?" Victor said, instantly scowling.

"You didn't hear?" Janine asked him.

"No," Victor said. "I was ... doing other things."

"It was reported today that Trever Mills was given a plea deal that allowed him to plead guilty to only simple assault," Chandler said.

Several others in the class groaned in disgust, apparently also hearing the news for the first time.

"It's a misdemeanor," Janine said in disgust. "It's not even a felony."

"All the charges against him are wrapped up, and he is being sentenced only to probation," Chandler said.

"He doesn't even have to register as a sex offender," Janine said.

"That's some bullshit," Loretta said.

"I'll say," Dapper Dan added.

"That sounds like an accurate summary," Chandler said, "but I'm afraid it's true."

"And that's it?" Victor asked. "Can't someone—the parents —object or something?"

"No," Chandler said. "It's final."

————

"That's what I heard," Lou said when Victor called the next day and asked him about Trever Mills's plea deal. "He must have some friends in high places."

"His father operates a mega-church and helped get the governor elected," Victor said.

"Well, there you go," Lou said, then added sarcastically, "Justice is served."

"That's revolting," Victor said.

"I know," Lou said, "but it happens all the time."

"Is there anything that can be done?" Victor asked.

"I'm not a lawyer, but no," Lou said. "Pleading guilty settles a case, and once it's settled, the person can't be prosecuted for the same actions again, no matter how lenient the sentence was or what new information is discovered."

Victor scoffed. "There must be something," he said. "What about if there are more victims?"

"It might be possible, but I've never seen it," Lou said. "I guess it depends on how the DA wrote up the plea deal." He made a thoughtful noise. "But I'd guess that a DA that gave him a deal this sweet also tied up the loose ends for him."

"Good grief," Victor said. "What bullshit."

"Bullshit like this happens pretty often, unfortunately," Lou said. "But, speaking of loose ends, I got a call from my friend in East St. Louis."

"Oh, yeah?" Victor said, shifting in his seat. "Is he still going to go out to that bar someday?"

"He says he already did, on Tuesday night."

"Oh, yeah?"

"Yeah," Lou said. He inhaled deeply, then sighed, shaking his head. "He said that Jordan Horn got into a fight with some idiot at the bar, and when my friend went to break it up, Jordan attacked him with a broken bottle."

"Really?" Victor said. "That sounds like a felony."

"Yeah, that's a felony, all right," Lou said. "You idiot."

"Well, I'd say justice is served on that one," Victor said.

"I guess," Lou said. "Let's just hope Jordan doesn't have friends in high places."

"Right," Victor said. "Or family."

———

Friday night, Victor took Janine out for dinner at a nice restaurant. It was the first time they had been anywhere on what could be considered a date. Afterward, they went back to her place to watch a movie. She made popcorn and they sat together on the couch, and it should have been a nice evening, but Victor was distracted.

Janine could tell. "What's on your mind?" she asked when the movie was finished and they went to the kitchen for fresh drinks.

Victor looked at her. His instinct was to evade the question, but he worked against it. "Trever Mills," he said.

Janine scoffed. "I know. I still can't believe that," she said, shaking her head. She turned to him with a genuine expression. "What do you think is going to happen?"

Victor raised his eyebrows and shook his head slowly. "I don't think anything can be done ..." He paused and averted his eyes, then added, "Legally."

"Legally," she repeated. "What do you mean? Do you think one of the victims ...?" She trailed off, frowning at the thought.

Victor shrugged. "Maybe, or one of their parents."

"Or a concerned citizen," Janine offered.

Victor shook his head and gave her a look of disgust. "This is one of the times when I wish that would happen, but it almost never does."

"Still," she said, "you never know."

They talked for a few more minutes about the case, but they had no new information, and they were merely rehashing the known injustices. The topic burned out after a while, and they fell into thoughtful silence again.

"Do you have any plans for Spring Break?" Victor asked her.

She shook her head. "No spring break from work," she said. "What about you?"

Victor shrugged. "I'm thinking about taking a little trip."

She made eye contact with him, her expression turning serious. "What for?"

Victor gave her a grim smile. "There's a problem I can fix."

"A problem," she repeated slowly, as though tasting the words. "Can't someone else fix it?"

He shook his head. "It doesn't look like it."

———

On Sunday, Victor tried to take a bus ride around the city to get a new perspective on everything and figure things out. He had forgotten that it was Sunday, though, and that meant the buses were running on a more limited schedule, so his thoughtful bus ride turned into a thoughtful walk.

He didn't mind. He could use the exercise.

In fact, he thought he had already made up his mind.

He was considering what the resolution of the Trever Mills case meant for the victims, for the world, and for the concept of justice.

Sometimes, Victor would hesitate to take action because there was a question of a person's guilt. That didn't apply here, though. Trever had pled guilty to the charges. He had *admitted* that he was guilty.

The next question was: was there justice for the victims? The obvious answer was no. No matter how you analyzed it, Trever had scarred many people, probably for life, and had gotten away with it. He may have gotten away with far worse. And all of it was now buried forever.

By any definition, that was not justice.

So the next question was: could some other entity, outside the legal system, intervene in this case to exact justice for the victims? Quite obviously, someone could.

But would anyone?

As far as he knew, he was the only person in the country with both the means and the opportunity to do what needed to be done. Lots of other people could be part of the criminal justice system. They had been. And they had failed. The only person who could get justice for all those victims was Victor.

He could do it.

Maybe, he *alone* could do it.

He already had ideas about how.

And if he was lucky, he could do it without killing anybody.

For once.

CHAPTER NINETEEN

Victor spent Sunday night at the condo, the one he still couldn't think of as *his*.

Monday morning, he called Janine before she left for work. "I'm going out of town for a few days," he said. "I have to help with that problem I told you about."

"*Have* to?" she asked, and added, "and you didn't really *tell* me about it."

"I'm sorry," he said, though without much conviction, because he wasn't, really. "We can talk about it when I get back."

Janine was quiet on the phone for a moment. "You have to go? *You* have to?"

He thought about this for a moment, almost as surprised at the word as she was. "I think I'm the only one who can," he said.

Victor couldn't see her reaction over the phone, but in her silence, he could feel that she wanted to ask him for more information about where he was going, and why. She also seemed to sense, however, that Victor would continue to avoid providing any details. "When will you be back?" she asked.

"I don't know," he said. "Probably in a couple of days, but maybe at the end of the week."

"Okay," she said, her tone grim. She seemed resolved that he was doing this. "Be careful."

"You know," he said after a moment, "this is dangerous. It's not likely, but there's always a chance that ... I might never be home."

She said nothing. The sounds of her getting ready in the background stopped, and she seemed to be absorbing the information. "Don't say that," she said, concern in her voice.

"It's not what I want to happen, and I'm certainly going to do everything I can to prevent it from happening, but sometimes ... that isn't enough."

Janine drew her breath in sharply on the phone.

"In fact," Victor added, "if things went very wrong, I might disappear, and no one might ever find out what happened to me."

She gasped. "Oh, my god," she said.

"That's not likely," he said, "and it was always the case when I was in the service, anyway, but I just wanted to make sure you knew that."

"Is this part of that undercover stuff you said you were doing with your friend Lou?" she asked.

"Kind of," Victor said. "Well, no, not really."

"Oh," Janine said. "Are you still involved with the military?" she asked. "Is this connected with that?"

"No," he said. "And I think this is much less dangerous. I'm sure everything is going to be all right, but I just wanted to say something, because you never know."

She was quiet for a moment. "It's possible that no one would ever know what happened to you?" she said. "How could that happen?"

"It's ... um ... independent work," Victor said.

"It sounds dangerous," Janine said.

"Not if it goes right," Victor said.

"And if it doesn't?"

"Well, that's why it's me," Victor said.

Janine was quite another moment, digesting the information. "I didn't know you were involved in things like this," she said.

I didn't realize that myself, Victor thought. He said, "I guess I am sometimes."

"Okay, Victor," she said. "Thanks for telling me." She paused a beat. "And be careful."

————

Later in the morning, Victor walked a few blocks to the edge of the downtown area where the rent was cheaper. It was almost noon, and the sun had warmed the street to the point that Victor was walking with his hands *not* in his jacket pockets. In fact, when the breeze blew just right, Victor could smell spring in the air, and if he looked *very* closely, he could see the green tips of new buds sprouting on some of the trees and bushes along the sidewalk.

On one of the quiet streets off the bus lines, Victor arrived at his destination: a small shop on the bottom floor of a building. The large front window had a pane in the bottom right temporarily replaced with a square of plywood, and in the top of the window was a simple lighted sign with a single word on it: *TRAVEL*. Victor pulled the door open and stepped inside.

The air inside the small storefront was only slightly warmer than the air outside, and it carried the odors of dust and old wood, together with the scent of the freshly printed pamphlets on the counter that stretched most of the way across the front part of the room. A thirty-something woman sat at a desk in the back corner of the room. She had straight black hair a little longer than shoulder-length, and she wore slacks and a jacket. She looked up when Victor came in and gave him a smile when she recognized him. "Hello," she said. He'd been here before, several times, but she didn't know his name, because he had never offered it.

"Hi there," Victor said. "I'm thinking of doing a little traveling."

"I thought you might be," she said. Her desk chair squeaked as she got to her feet and came to the counter. "By air this time, or ..."

Victor was already shaking his head. "The bus again," he said. "I like the bus."

"Of course," she said. "Where will you be going this time?"

As she reached the counter, Victor's nostrils caught the scent of clean laundry, and he was momentarily almost distracted. He smiled. "I'm going to visit an acquaintance."

"A friend?" she asked. She squinted her eyes, trying to remember. "Was it Kansas City?"

Outward, Victor tried to give no reaction to the statement, but inside, he was cringing. If she could remember him, and where he'd been traveling, he was failing at being nondescript and unmemorable. Maybe it was time to find another travel agent. Still, this one was close. Besides, she was sweet, and she seemed to need the money, and she smelled ... good. "No, a different acquaintance this time," he said. "I was thinking Joplin."

"Oh," she said with a smile. "A short trip. Driving might be better. Have you considered that? I could get you a good rate on a rental car."

"No, thank you," Victor said. "I like the bus."

She opened her mouth to speak, then made brief eye

contact with Victor before turning to a file cabinet behind the counter. "Of course," she said, "the bus for you."

With a shock of insult, Victor realized that she must think that he *couldn't* drive—that his license had been revoked or that he'd never learned in the first place. Though that was insulting, he gritted his teeth and said nothing while she got out her book of bus schedules and tickets. The less she knew about him—and the more she thought she knew about him that was wrong—the better.

———

After securing the bus ticket, Victor walked to Spence's shop. As he walked, he could smell the spring in the air even more, and he could feel it lifting his spirits. The world was refreshing with new life and new relationships, and for the first time in a long time, he was taking part in it himself. He couldn't wait for his current cleaning project to be done so he could get back to doing what animals do in the springtime.

For a fraction of an instant, his mind tried to wonder whether this cleaning project was necessary, but he had already resolved the matter. People wanted it done. He would not be happy until it was done. He was the only one who could do it. He was doing it. End of story.

Spence's shop was not far from the travel agent's shop, but it was past noon by the time he got there. He hoped Spence was not out to lunch, and he was not, at least, not *out* to lunch.

"Good afternoon, Mr. Storm," Spence said as Victor entered the shop. He was standing at the display case in the back, eating a submarine sandwich, and he wrapped it back in its paper wrapper and wiped his hands on a napkin before shaking Victor's hand.

"Hello, Spence," Victor said. He didn't remember how

Spence knew his full name, and he rather wished now that he didn't, but that was a problem for another day.

"Was your friend happy to get his identification back?" Spence asked.

Victor gave him a blank look. "I'm sorry, Spence," he said. "I don't know what you're talking about."

"I'm sorry. That's my mistake," Spence said. "I was thinking of someone else, of course."

"Of course," Victor said, smiling again.

"So, what brings you to my shop on this fine spring day?" Spence asked.

"I have a friend who lost his backup gun," Victor said.

"Is that so?" Spence asked.

"It is," Victor said, "and he's heartbroken, because this was a truly great backup gun, small, reliable, and he's afraid he won't be able to get it back because it wasn't registered."

"It wasn't registered?" Spence asked.

"No," Victor said. "He couldn't get it registered because it didn't have a serial number on it."

"Someone filed off the serial number?"

Victor shook his head. "He doesn't know *how* it happened. He just knows that it never had a serial number on it as far as he knows."

"I see," Spence said.

"Yeah, so, my friend lives around here, and he can't find it, so he's thinking maybe that someone found it and turned it in to a shop like this one."

"Turned it in?" Spence asked. "I see, because—"

"Because it would be illegal to sell a gun without a serial number," Victor said.

Spence nodded. "I can see how that might happen."

"So," Victor said, "my friend asked me to check to see if any shops had it. Like I said, he's heartbroken."

"Heartbroken," Spence repeated, still nodding.

"Yeah," Victor said. "And he'd pay a big reward to get it back."

"Well, I certainly understand an emotional attachment to firearms," he said. "Let me see if I have anything like that in my lost and found."

―――――

Victor returned to the condo to get ready for his trip.

Then he had an idea.

He knew it wasn't a good idea, but before he could stop himself, he had dialed Angelina's number. It was after dinner time in North Carolina, and as the phone rang, he wondered whether that made it more or less likely that she would answer the phone, more or less likely that she would be busy.

He was surprised when she answered the phone on the second ring.

"The girls are getting ready for bed," she said, "but you can talk to them for a few minutes."

He bristled at the suggestion that he needed her *permission* to talk to his own daughters, but he shoved that thought aside for the moment. "Actually," he said, "I was hoping to talk to you."

He heard her take a deep breath. "About what? Something in the divorce papers?"

"No, well, kind of, I guess," he said. He took a deep breath himself. "Actually, I was wondering if maybe it's too soon to fill them out."

Angelina groaned. "Victor, we've been over this," she said. "It's been three ye—"

"It's only been two," he said, "but that's not what I mean."

She groaned again. "What do you mean, then?"

"I'm talking about us, being together," he said. "Did we try hard enough to make it work?"

She made a noise into the phone, something between a scoff and a sob. "*I* did," she said. "*I* was there. I kept our house together. I took care of our daughters—"

"But with *us*," he said. "I'm just wondering if we've done enough to make sure that we *can't* be married, that divorce really is the answer."

Angelina sighed into the phone. "Have you changed things?" she asked.

"I think so," he said. "I'm taking classes."

"But are you still getting into fights in bars? Are you still having those dreams?" Her voice held tones of frustration, disappointment, and acceptance in equal measures.

"I—That's not the point," Victor said. "Lou says I can go to the VA..." He trailed off, not sure what he was arguing now.

"*Have* you gone to the VA?" she asked.

Victor said nothing. A long moment passed.

On Angelina's end of the line, he heard the voice of one of his daughters in the background. There was a rustle, then Angelina was back on the line. "I have to go," she said. "Is there something more? Do you want to talk to the girls?"

Victor closed his eyes. "I can't right now," he said. "I have to go, too."

CHAPTER TWENTY

Monday evening, although he was headed to Dallas, Victor really did go to Joplin. He packed a simple bag, loading a duffel bag he found in a thrift store with some cash, a few other necessities, and some dollar-store things like tape and rope that might come in handy. Because he was taking the bus, he didn't have to consider security screenings, and because he was paying cash, he could get by taking no credit cards, just a simple identification card.

The card didn't have his real name on it, and the picture didn't look like him, but that hardly mattered. He could pass it off as his own or one he found, whatever worked best for whatever came up.

Shortly after sunset, he left his condo and walked to a city bus line not in front of his condo building, then took the city bus to the Greyhound station, which was teeming with activity. He was always surprised at how busy the station was until he remembered that it was a central point connecting the east side of the country with the west side.

He already had his ticket, so he had no need to go to the counter or to talk to anyone. Instead, he merely walked down the line of gates and found the one for Joplin, where the bus was getting ready to depart. Victor joined the queue of boarding passengers, climbed the stairs, and gave his ticket to a driver who looked well-rested and ready to drive through the night. The sound of shoes on the solid floor of the bus and the scent of the conditioned air inside the bus roused memories in him and brought him a sense of peace, and of being alive.

The passengers who had boarded ahead of him found empty seats and stuffed their bags into the overhead compartments. The other passengers were waiting for the bus to leave, passing the time reading or sleeping or, in one case, trying to keep a toddler entertained. Victor walked down the aisle and took a window seat in the back of the bus, then settled in with his duffel bag on his lap.

The bus departed on time, a few minutes after Victor boarded, and Victor watched as the bus rumbled onto the highway and out toward the sunset and the familiar landmarks of downtown St. Louis slipped into the past. Before long, they were out of the city and into the darkness, and Victor could see a panoply of shimmering stars in the sky. It made him feel very small, completely insignificant, and somehow, inexplicably, completely wrong.

He tried to ignore it.

This route went through Joplin, Missouri, and on through Oklahoma, Texas, New Mexico, and Arizona on its way to the coast of California. It was a popular route, and the bus had few empty seats. Though someone sat in the seat next to him, Victor minded his own business and watched the blackness out the window as the bus rolled down the highway.

He tried to think about the condo, and what furniture they still had to move to Samantha's. He tried to think about his wife, and what had made her leave, and how he might make things different. He thought about his daughters and the world they would grow up and live their lives in.

He tried not to think about where he was going and what it meant for him. It wasn't time yet.

A few hours later, shortly after midnight, the bus arrived at the station in Joplin. Victor shouldered the thrift-store bag and got off the bus. This time, he did go into the station, where he gave a sleepy-eyed clerk cash for another one-way ticket, this time to Dallas. He was lucky. The bus was leaving in less than an hour.

While he waited for the bus, Victor stood outside and smoked a cigarette. Outside the bus station, he could smell the strong odors of diesel exhaust and heavy machinery oil. His brain associated the scents with military bases and equipment, and he liked it. It felt like home.

The bus to Dallas had a lot of cowboy hats, which made Victor smile. He idly thought about getting one for himself, and he decided he would if he found a small place selling them along the way.

Once again, he took a window seat as far back as possible and kept to himself.

———

As the bus rumbled through the night, Victor found himself thinking about his marriage. Again.

By now, he knew that getting divorced was the right thing to do. Angelina had been gone two years—almost three. She was moving on with her life, and that was the right thing for her to do.

He, however, hadn't changed. He hadn't *been able* to change. He liked to think of himself as powerful, capable of doing anything. But he hadn't been able to change himself. He still had the bad dreams, and he still couldn't bring himself to do anything about them. He was still looking for trouble, and finding it.

Still, though, he realized that he *had* been able to make one change: he had a girlfriend. That change, though, had moved him further from reconciliation with his wife, not closer.

He knew that, probably, the right thing to do was to give his wife the divorce she wanted.

But that would mean admitting that he was powerless to change himself, the thing he should have the *most* control over. Even worse, it would mean breaking a sacred promise. He had promised Angelina, more than a decade and a half ago, that he would be there for her, always. Whatever he thought of religion, he considered that a sacred promise. If he was unable to control himself, and he was unable to keep his most sacred promises, what good could he be to anyone, ever?

Those were the thoughts ravaging his brain as the bus rolled through the night, and though his eyes pierced the darkness at the ordinary world outside the window, he found no answers.

The bus made several stops at small towns in Oklahoma and Texas along the way, and in the early part of the trip, Victor got out and smoked when he could. Later, as the night grew longer, he dozed in his seat with his bag on his lap.

Before he knew it, the sun was coming up, and the bus was rolling through the Dallas metropolitan area.

Now, it was time to think again about what he was doing, and whether it was a good idea. He didn't have to think long.

He still hadn't changed his mind.

It was time to do what only he could do.

Somehow.

In Dallas, Victor continued to move in a way designed to leave the smallest imprint of himself in the transportation systems and the memories of the people around him. That meant, to the best extent possible, he avoided areas watched by security cameras, he made no requests that would stick out in the minds of bus or taxi drivers, and he interacted with the fewest number of people possible.

When the bus stopped at the Dallas station, he left the bus station without hesitation, walked down the street to the city bus stop not closest to the bus station, and climbed aboard a bus headed downtown. Although he could not avoid all the security cameras and personal interaction, this style of movement made him practically invisible.

Dallas was warmer than St. Louis had been, but it was still chilly. The air smelled dry and dusty, but even so, it held the unmistakable scent of spring.

On the city bus, Victor picked up a schedule book from a rack behind the driver, then sat in the back and opened it to the map section. Before leaving St. Louis, he had researched the location of the Trinity River Christian Outreach, and though it was of course not printed on the bus maps, he was easily able to locate where it would be and identify the routes to get there. You didn't need weeks of orienteering instruction to plan a route on a bus map, but it didn't hurt.

Downtown, Victor got off the bus and walked around until he found a suitable small motel, the kind where you slide your registration card and money in a tray under a pane of bullet-proof glass to a clerk watching the clock and tapping his cigarette into an ashtray on the desk, and he checked in paying cash. The name he gave matched neither the name on his birth certificate nor the name on the identification card in his bag, but the motel clerk, a guy with greasy black hair and thick glasses, did not seem interested in the slightest.

Victor went to the room and found what he had expected: cigarette burns on the carpet and the table by the window and the noisy air conditioner, a queen bed with a stained comforter, a battered wooden dresser with an old television bolted onto it, and scratchy white towels. It was perfect for his intentions. He took a shower to wash off the grit from his bus rides, then took a nap on top of the comforter until mid-afternoon.

He dressed again, then went down the street to get an ordinary dinner at a chain restaurant that didn't have waitresses. The food wasn't great, but it would do.

Back in the motel room, Victor found a set of phone books. The research his class had done on Trever Mills had told him that Trever still lived at the church, presumably in a room at his father's mansion. In fact, though he was on leave, he still had a job at the outreach center, and it seemed his father had hope that he would follow in his footsteps. What they had not established, however, was whether the family's mansion was on the grounds of the church, or if it was somewhere else. Given Trever's father's evident lust for money, Victor thought it likely would be in one of the swanky new developments in the Dallas suburbs.

The phone books, however, suggested the church and the family mansion were neighbors, if not directly adjacent. The church had a listing in the yellow pages, and Trever's father Edmond Mills was listed in the white pages, with a street address only a few digits higher than that of the church. Surprisingly, Victor found a number for a *T. Mills*, also at the same address. This must be Trever, the thought, but he had not expected it to be listed.

Victor made a mental note of the addresses, but did not write them down. He still had the bus system book, and he mapped out a route to get there. The trip would take the better part of an hour and a half, but he'd only have to transfer buses once. And if he left right away, he would get there right after sundown, and he'd still have plenty of time to catch the reverse buses back.

Fortunately, he still had his shoes on. He donned the jacket he'd found in the thrift store with the duffel bag, stuffed the gear from the duffel bag into various carrying places, and left, tucking the motel room key behind a brick in the planter by the parking lot on his way to the bus.

CHAPTER TWENTY-ONE

The last light was draining from the sky as Victor arrived at the Trinity River Christian Outreach. The road it was on went through marshes, and the enormous campus was built on reclaimed swamp land. Victor could see tall reeds along the sides of the property, and enormous trees were visible in the swampland in the back.

The church itself was a massive structure of stained glass and stucco, with curved walls, low-angled rooftops, and a pitched steeple thrusting skyward, and road-ward, in the center. A huge parking lot sat to the right side of the church, with a two-story building behind it with a walkway on the second floor and rows of doors visible on both. The building's shape and signage indicated it was an administrative building.

On the left side of the church, set back a little farther from the road, was an enormous mansion, with tall, white columns across its front, a wrap-around porch, an entryway of arched wooden double doors, and a balcony at the top of the arches.

With the landscape rapidly growing darker, Victor walked down the road past the building, then turned and walked along a wire fence at the edge of the property line to the back of the campus. He tried to look confident and act disinterested in the church and the campus, perhaps passing himself off as a neighbor addressing something on his own property, or something like that. He wondered if he might have been wiser to have worn a safety vest and carried a clipboard, or perhaps to wear a hunting cap and carry a rifle, to avoid attracting undue attention. If someone did come his way, he'd pass himself off as a neighbor looking for a lost puppy, but it would be better not to attract attention in the first place.

As he advanced toward the far corner of the perimeter fence, Victor could see the back side of the mansion, as well as another set of buildings at the edge of the reclaimed swamp. These buildings were dark, a collection of cabins, common rooms, dormitories, a gazebo, and a barn, and he recognized what they must be: the summer camp.

Still seeing no one and sensing that he was undetected, Victor lowered himself to a crouch and watched the scene, wondering what to do next. It was still about seven in the evening, but he'd have to leave by nine to catch the bus back to town. If he was going to find Trever tonight, he was going to have to do it fast, and probably get a little lucky.

He waited a few more minutes watching the various buildings, but saw nothing promising. There were a few lights on in the house, but he couldn't see any distinct movement, and he didn't see anything to indicate where Trever might be, or even if he was here at all. Fortunately, he didn't see anyone else about on the campus grounds, either. He had been concerned about caretakers, or interns, or monks, or something, but none of those worries were panning out. He seemed to be alone outside.

Several more minutes passed, and finally, he could wait no more. He had to find Trever. Ducking low, he slipped through the fence and hurried across the lawn to the back corner of the mansion, still trying to make his movements plausibly those of someone looking for a lost puppy. He figured the room on the front of the building, upstairs with the big balcony, had to be the master bedroom. The secondary bedrooms would probably be on the back of the building somewhere. Victor could peek in through the windows, at least through the ones on the ground floor, and hopefully, he'd be able to locate Trever. If he couldn't, he'd have to slip inside somehow and look upstairs and in the rest of the house. That would be much more dangerous, but at least there was a door on the back of the house, and the wrap-around porch made it more likely that someone would leave a side or back entrance unlocked, so he had some hope of being able to do it at all.

Most of the rooms along the back of the house had no lights on inside. Giving up any remaining pretense of looking for a puppy, Victor crept closer and looked into them all anyway. The ones he could see inside were, indeed, bedrooms, and they had the impersonal look of guest bedrooms to boot. Finally, at the far side of the house, he realized he was going to have to do something more drastic.

Victor had a lot of ideas for creating a disturbance large enough to get people out of the house, but before he could begin making a plan, he heard the back door open. Instantly, he dropped to the ground and flattened himself against the wooden lattice at the bottom of the porch. The thought ran through his head that his lost puppy ploy might have still worked, but by then it was too late.

Victor heard the back screen door swing open, then bang closed as footsteps crossed the wooden porch to the stairs. A young man came into view as he descended the steps and headed back to the summer camp buildings.

The young man was slender, with brown hair, and even

from the side and in the dim light, Victor recognized him at once: Trever Mills.

Feeling a rush of adrenaline, Victor scrambled as quietly as he could around the corner of the porch, then peeked back at Trever. Apparently lost in his own thoughts, the young man didn't seem to have heard a thing.

As Victor watched, Trever walked down the slightly sloped yard to the camp buildings, where he walked directly to the front door of the cabins. There, he paused long enough to take a brief look around himself at the landscape, then he opened the door and went inside.

A light came on in the cabin, then another. Several minutes passed, and Victor realized that Trever must be living in one of the cabins.

By himself.

This was perfect.

Victor looked at his watch again. He still had a little more than an hour to make it back to the last bus. Time would probably be tight, but he thought he would make it.

And he knew now what he was going to do.

Victor shifted himself into a position with his feet under him, tipped his head out slightly, and listened for sounds coming from inside the house. He could hear the noises of the insects in the swamp getting stirred up by the sunset, and he could hear the distant growl of a truck passing on the road out front, but he could hear nothing from inside the house. No television, no music, no voices, nothing. He wondered if Trever had been alone in the house the whole time. If he was, that meant people might be returning at any moment. He had to get busy.

Victor rose to a full standing position. If someone *was* here to observe him, he wanted to appear matter-of-fact, normal, not like an intruder. He strode toward the cabin, and he looked around as he walked, trying to seem as though he was appreciating the dusk, not snooping. He had no idea if someone saw him and thought nothing about him. Pretty much the whole point in doing it was to never know if it had needed to be done.

Another car passed on the road out front, but he saw no other sign of people. His shoes made a whisking sound in the grass as he walked, and with the fading light, the earthy moist odors of the swamp seemed to be more pronounced.

Victor reached the cabin, stepped up onto a small wooden porch in front of the door, took a deep breath, and knocked.

Footsteps sounded inside the cabin, coming close, then the door swung open. Maybe someone else was on the property, because Trever answered the door with a smile as though he was expecting someone. He was about the same height as Victor—six feet tall—but was more wiry. He wore a collared shirt and khaki slacks, and Victor caught the scent of cologne.

At the sight of Victor, the expression on Trevor's face instantly went from happiness to disappointment to suspicion.

Before Trever could react, however, Victor lunged forward, gripped Trever's collar in one hand and his elbow with the other, then shoved him back into the room and kicked the door closed. The doorway opened into a sitting area with a small television on a stand to the left of the door, and two chairs and a couch with a trunk positioned between them like a coffee table.

"Jesus," Trever said, more annoyed than scared. "What is this?"

Victor kept pushing Trever backward, keeping him off balance until his feet bumped against the couch and he fell to a sitting position on the cushions.

"What the *fuck?!*" Trever said, his face suddenly red.

Victor shoved Trever back into the cushions of the couch, then let go of his collar and elbow, stepped back, and took a quick glance around. To the right was the kitchen area, and next to that a door to a bathroom. In the back behind the couch, an open doorway showed a room where a light Victor couldn't see revealed a twin bed. On the left, behind the chairs, another open door led to a darkened room that held at least one set of bunk beds. The light in this room came from a lamp on a table between the end of the couch and the chairs.

Trever should have been afraid, but he didn't seem to be. He looked confused more than anything. "What the fuck is this?" he demanded.

Victor had a barely controllable urge to strike Trever in the nose with his elbow, or the heel of his hand. Trever had worn a condescending smirk in every picture of him Victor had seen, but in person, it was ten times worse. He exuded arrogance. He was a very bad person who thought himself better than very good people, which made Victor want to put him in his place.

And that's what he was here for.

"Are you another reporter?" Trever said, smoothing down his shirt where Victor had grabbed him. "God, why can't you guys leave me alone."

"I'm not a reporter," Victor said quietly.

Trever tensed at Victor's words, finally seeming to sense Victor was something different. "What are you then?" he asked. "A stalker? A thrill-seeker?" The tone in his voice suggested he was hoping Victor was one of those, something he knew how to handle.

"No," Victor said. He inhaled slowly, staring directly at Trever. "I'm here to get justice for the people you hurt."

Trever snorted, but Victor saw fear in his eye. He seemed

to have finally realized that he was in danger, and he was struggling to keep his composure. "What?" he said. "Don't you
watch the news? That's already been done."

"Not completely," Victor said. "I want you to make a full
public confession."

"Are you an idiot?" Trever asked. "I pled guilty. Those
charges are done, and I'm paying what everyone thinks is a
very fair price for my crimes." He shook his head at Victor,
smirking again. "It's over. I can't be prosecuted for them again,
not even if I confess to every detail on live TV."

"That's not what I want you to confess to," Victor said.
"I'm talking about Kolby French."

Trever's face paled, and he jerked his head. "I don't know
anything about that, and even if I did, I've already pleaded
guilty."

"Not to murder," Victor said. "Not to Kolby French."

"You're crazy," Trever said. "I'm not going to do that."

"Yes, you are," Victor said, "or I'm going to come back here
and kill you."

"What?" Trever said, a tremble in his voice now. "You can't.
That's not—that's not *legal*."

"Yes, I can. I'm not here to enforce the law; I'm here for
justice," Victor said. "And don't think you can run away, either.
I will always be able to find you. This is what I do. This is my
job."

Trever made a whimpering noise. "I can't be convicted if
I'm forced to confess."

"Yes, you can," Victor said. "I'm not a cop, and you're going
to provide details that only you would know." Victor shrugged.
"That's your choice: confess and go to prison, or don't, and I
will kill you." He smiled and shook his head. "Those are your
only two options."

Trever looked terrified, and for a change, he said nothing.

Victor stepped backward to the door and opened it without taking his eyes off Trever. "Don't mess this up, Trever," Victor said. "Do it tomorrow, or I'll be back."

CHAPTER TWENTY-TWO

Back at the motel room, Victor sat in the chair by the bed and felt dismal. Though he had spent an hour after he left Trever working through the darkness back to the road, and another hour on the bus coming back downtown, he could still feel the effects of the adrenaline.

But worse than that, he was sure he had wasted his time.

There was no way Trever was going to confess. He was a spoiled rich kid, used to getting his way, used to getting away with everything, *raised* to believe he was better than everyone else. Was he going to confess, as Victor had demanded?

Of course not.

Victor stripped down and took a shower in the dingy bathroom. The tile was chipped, the grout dirty, and the soap tiny, but the water was hot and it felt good running down the back of his neck. He liked to think of himself as a smooth operator, but standing under the water, he could feel knots of tension in his shoulders. He rolled his head around on his neck, loosening his neck muscles, and tried not to assume that the worst was going to happen.

It wasn't easy, though. His plan now felt foolish, maybe even dumb, destined to not only fail but to actively make things worse.

The right thing, probably, would have been to simply kill Trever and leave. But was that something he could have done? Even when confronting his own parents' killer, Victor had only resorted to murder as an absolute last resort.

He had steered the man into it, but still, last resort.

This time, though, he had given Trever a chance to fight back. And he sensed that Trever *would* fight back. He didn't know how, but somehow.

So now, it would be a fight.

And still, Victor couldn't walk away.

The next day, Victor paid for another night at the motel and tried not to think about what was going to happen. After a fast-food breakfast, he took the bus to the public library and explored their collections for several hours. He was fascinated by the map section and the archive of historical books, and he wished he had more time to browse them, but that would have to wait for another day.

Mid-afternoon, Victor visited another fast-food place for an early dinner. Later, as the sun was going down, Victor turned on the television. He figured that if Trever Mills had confessed, it would be a major story carried by all the local stations. So, he caught the early evening news and the regular evening news, and he flipped back and forth on all the local channels to make sure he saw all the big stories.

He was not surprised at all to see that Trever Mills was not one of them.

So, Trever had made his decision, and, unfortunately, it was now time for Victor to make his. Was he going to go and kill this young man in cold blood, as he had promised? Or was he going to do something else? And if so, what?

Right off, Victor knew he did not *want* to kill Trever. He had had enough of killing. Too much. He could kill to protect his family, or in self-defense, probably, but only as a reluctant last resort.

Despite his tough talk, it seemed he was unlikely to be able to walk the walk. Had Trever sensed this weakness? Maybe.

Victor considered his options.

One choice was to simply go home. Now that Victor had confronted Trever and promised to kill him, maybe Trever would always be looking over his shoulder and perpetually on his best behavior. Maybe, but that seemed far-fetched.

Another option would be to go and kill Trever as he had promised. That one, though, seemed like a non-starter. He didn't want to be a simple killer.

So, what then?

He realized that he had to go and confront Trever. Maybe he could tell Trever that he would be watching him and that he was going to kill him when he least expected it. That didn't sound very good, but maybe he could think of something better on the way.

Or, maybe he'd get lucky and Trever would try to kill him first and he'd have to kill him in self-defense.

It occurred to Victor that none of these thoughts were rational, and were quite possibly insane. He shook his head in disappointment at himself.

Because he was going to do it anyway.

———

Once again, Victor packed his things, hid the key, and got on the bus. As he had the day before, he again transferred to another bus to complete the ride out to the Trinity River Christian Outreach. Not wanting to arrive at the same time as the day before, he took the next later bus. It would leave him less time to finish whatever he was going to do and to catch the return bus, but if things went poorly, he might not want to be seen on the returning bus at all. He had the bus map and schedule with him for that possibility, in which he'd walk to catch a bus on a different nearby line if he could, or he'd hike all the way back if he couldn't.

This time, he rode past the church on the bus. He watched carefully as the bus rumbled by, expecting to see a police presence, or ... something.

Instead, it looked just the same as the night before, except with the sun already beginning to slip below the western horizon.

Victor got off the bus at the stop past the church, walked back to the grounds, and stopped at the corner of the property where the fence went back from the road. He kept a low profile and concealed himself in the darkness, studying the church, the house, and the summer camp cabins for a few moments. He could see no activity at the church. A black sedan sat parked at the end of the driveway at the back of the house, and he didn't think that had been there the night before, but he couldn't be sure. At any rate, if Trever had called the police or other backup, there would surely be many new cars, and there was nothing of the sort.

Victor could again see no activity in the house, either. There seemed to be a light on downstairs on the right, but that looked like a kitchen light or something left on for someone's return, not like a lamp someone was using to read by or something. He could see no movement, and he saw no lights on upstairs at all.

At the camp area, the one cabin appeared to have the same lights on as before. Perhaps Trever had fled in fear and not returned. Victor had a feeling, though, that he was still there.

Waiting for him.

Could Trever have ignored Victor completely? If he had, Victor still had no real idea what he was going to do about it. He'd think of something, though.

Victor crept along the fence back to the summer camp buildings, breathing through his nose and trying to ignore the mosquitos.

Unlike the previous night, when he made little effort to conceal himself, he ducked low when he moved, crouched when he stopped, and stayed out of sight as much as possible. The sun had finished disappearing from the sky, but even moving cautiously and keeping careful watch, he covered the ground quickly.

He reached the clearing with the camp buildings, then crept around to the back of Trever's cabin, staying concealed in the foliage at the edge of the clearing. He crossed the paths of several trails leading into the swamp, presumably for nature hikes for the campers. Much of the light had drained from the sky, and at the edge of the swamp, the trees and vines made the terrain even darker. Victor was increasingly unable to avoid stepping on twigs and branches as he moved, but as the darkness grew, he felt more comfortable moving into the edge of the clearing.

As he neared the cabin, Victor listened even more intently for sounds of activity. He heard nothing. He thought he could see the lights inside the cabin flickering a little, as though a television was on, but he couldn't hear anything. The curtains were closed across the windows. He hadn't been around to the back side of the cabin the previous night, so he didn't know if this was a precaution taken against him, but it seemed like one. If drawn curtains were Trever's best defense, he was in big trouble.

Victor moved to the cabin, flattened himself against the

wall, then slipped around the corner from the back to the right side. This position left him exposed to the house and parts of the church, but he saw no activity there. Stepping gingerly, he moved to the window, where he was surprised to see the curtains open.

Moving cautiously, Victor peeked inside. Trever was sitting on the couch watching television. From here, he could have been keeping a close eye on the door and the front window, but he didn't appear to be. Instead, he appeared to be engrossed in whatever was on the television and completely unconcerned about Victor or anything else in the world.

Keeping himself out of view, Victor examined the inside of the cabin. He could see a glass with a bubbly liquid in it on the table with the lamp on it beside Trever, but nothing else. He could see no guns or weapons of any kind anywhere in the cabin, not so much as a knife for whittling.

Trever seemed not to have believed Victor at all.

That was going to be a mistake.

Victor went back to the front door of the cabin. Last night, he had knocked, but this time he didn't want to give himself away. He gripped the door handle lightly and tested it. Amazingly, it was unlocked. Victor scoffed. Trever had been scared to the point of trembling with fear by the time Victor left the previous night, but apparently, he had been able to recover himself enough to achieve a state of total denial. Amazing.

Victor took a deep breath, twisted the door handle, and burst into the room.

"What the fuck, dude?" Trever said, turning to him. "I'm watching TV."

The television was on a stand in front of the window. Victor reached over and turned it off. Again, despite what he'd seen he expected Trever to charge at him when he reached for the television, or to do *something*—anything at all. Instead, Trever merely sat on the couch, smirking at him.

Victor turned to him. "I watched the news today," he said. "You weren't on it."

"I've been on it a lot lately," Trever said. "I wanted to take the night off."

"Well, unfortunately, Trever, I wasn't joking," Victor said. "That was your one chance, and you blew it."

"I didn't blow anything," Trever said. "Get the fuck out of here, or I'll bury *you* in the swamp."

Victor looked at him. Trever was smirking. He had chosen his words deliberately. He was taunting Victor with what had happened to Kolby French. "Get up, Trever," Victor said, his mouth feeling dry. "Time for games is over."

Trever stared at him, not smiling at all now. "You don't get it, do you?" he said. "You don't have any idea who the fuck you're messing with."

"You're an arrogant punk," Victor said. "I've known hundreds just like you."

Trever scoffed. "Not like me, you haven't," he said. "I've got something special that I'm sure none of your other boyfriends had."

"What's that?" Victor asked.

Trever smiled again. "I'm rich enough to buy a gun," he said. Suddenly, he darted forward, reaching for the cushions at the side of the couch by the lamp.

He was too far away, though. Victor beat him to the end of the couch, pushed Trever back easily, and lifted the cushion.

There was nothing underneath but some broken bits of brown pretzel and yellow popcorn.

Victor looked back at Trever and let the cushion go.

A man had come out of the bedroom where the bunk beds

were, one of the rooms where the curtains had been drawn. He was holding a pistol and pointing it at Victor.

Trevor straightened and stepped back, combing the hair back off his forehead with his fingers. "I'm sorry," he said, smirking like an idiot. "Did I say *buy* a gun? I meant *hire* a gun."

CHAPTER TWENTY-THREE

Victor froze. The gunman didn't look like a pro. He appeared to be about Trever's age or maybe a little younger. He was slender, with dark brown hair in a bowl cut and a thin black mustache that looked like the product of a lot of effort. He looked scared. His blue eyes looked close to panic, and he had his finger on the trigger in a way that suggested he might *accidentally* pull it. "Take it easy," Victor said. "Everybody just calm down."

"Oh, *now* you want to calm down, right?" Trever said. "You ain't so big now, are you?"

"I never said I was big," Victor said, not taking his eyes off the gunman. "I said I was going to kill you, and I still am."

"You idiot," Trever said with a giddy laugh. "You don't even know you got played." He stood up and approached Victor. "Give me your gun," he said.

"What makes you think I have a gun?" Victor asked.

"Of course, you have a gun," Trever said.

"If he had a gun, why didn't he have it out?" asked the gunman.

"Shut up, Doug," Trever said. He turned back to Victor.

"I'm going to give you to the count of three, and if you haven't given me your gun, Doug is going to shoot you." He looked at Doug, then back at Victor. "One!"

Victor held up a hand. Doug looked terrified. He was going to shoot way before Trever got to three. "Hold on," he said. "I've got it right here," he said. He reached for his jacket pocket. "Easy, now," he said.

"*I'll* get it," Trever said. He stepped forward, yanked the corner of Victor's jacket open, and pulled the gun out. Satisfied the pocket was empty, he reached for the other side of the jacket and shook that pocket as well, then stepped back with a smile. "We got you now, asshole," he said. "You keep your hands up where I can see them, and let's go for a walk."

Very slowly, Victor turned around, and Trever pushed him in the back toward the door. "Easy, now," Victor said. "You're in charge here. We're doing what you want. There's no rush."

Victor opened the door, and Trever pushed him out at the point of the gun he'd taken from him. Victor sneaked a glance over at the house and church. Despite being disarmed, though, he still was hoping they weren't seen.

"You looking for help?" Trever said, apparently noticing that Victor had looked over at the church. He laughed. "There's no help over there," he said. "They're on sabbatical." He stopped laughing. "Not even Jesus can help you now."

"I don't need help," Victor said. "I've got everything under control."

"Yeah, right you do," Trever said. "That way."

Victor felt the gun jab him in the back, pushing him toward the path that led into the swamp.

"We should make him get in his car and take him far away from here," Doug said.

"We don't know where his car is," Trever said.

"I parked it close by, but you'll never find it," Victor said, turning to look at Trever. "Someone else is going to see it, though, and they'll come looking for me."

Trever looked at him, eyes narrowed in thought, then he chuckled. "We'll take care of it later," he said. "Everything disappears in the swamp." He shoved the gun into Victor's back again. "Get going."

They reached the edge of the clearing, where weeds had been trampled into the black earth, making a path that led into the murky darkness of the swamp. The night insects and animals, which had been revved up in their sundown sounds, grew quiet around them as they approached.

Victor assessed his situation as they stepped onto the path, into the solitude of the swamp. Things looked grim. For Trever. He might think he had an advantage in this swampy terrain, in the darkness, away from any witnesses, but he didn't. "You should have confessed, Trever," he said.

"I *did* confess," Trever said. "I got probation." He laughed. "I've certainly learned my lesson."

"Even running away would have been better," Victor said.

"You're the one that should have run away," Trever said. "You never should have come back."

They continued down the path for forty or fifty yards. The path got weedier and soggier the further Victor walked. The swamp smelled cold, and the branches of the trees around them stood out black against the starry sky.

The path led to the right around a corner with a big, weedy pool on the left-hand side. "Stop right here," Trever said to Victor. "Turn around."

Victor stopped and turned to face Trever and Doug. He still had his hands raised, but only about halfway. Doug's eyes were wide with fear, and even Trever seemed jumpy.

"Right there," Trever said to Doug. "Do it, Doug."

"What?" Doug said.

"Shoot him," Trever said, excitement in his voice. "Just like we talked about. Shoot him."

"I—I thought you were going to," Doug said.

"You're going to do it," Trever said. "For me."

"O—okay," Doug said. He turned back to Victor, his hand shaking more than ever.

"You don't have to do this, Doug," Victor said.

"Yes, you do," Trever said. "Shoot him."

"Shut up," Doug said to everyone. "I will." He steadied the gun at Victor.

Victor gave them a surprised look. "You can't shoot me with that," Victor said to Doug. "Has that been like that the whole time?" He gave a dry laugh. "Seriously?"

"What are you talking about?" Doug asked.

With his right hand, Victor pointed in the direction of the gun. "You still have the safety on," he said.

"Don't—" Trever started to say, but it was too late.

Doug looked at the gun where Victor was pointing.

And at the same time, Victor swung his left fist down onto the other side of the gun. The blow pounded his knuckles into the back of Doug's hand. The gun went flying. Doug's arm flew out of control toward Trever's face.

Doug squealed.

Trever howled and ducked out of the way.

The gun flew through the air and landed in the reeds at the edge of the pool.

Doug scrambled for it as Victor turned to Trever. Before Trever could recover and get Victor's gun back in position for a shot, Victor kicked at his head. He missed, but the kick kept Trever from aiming. Victor kicked again, this time connecting with Trever's upper arm. Trever let out a shout of rage, turned, and ran back down the path.

Victor let him go for the moment and turned back to

Doug, who was scrambling in the weeds looking for the gun. Victor charged toward him, but Doug let out a cry of delight and pounced on the gun, grabbing it with both hands. He turned and aimed at Victor, who managed to hurl himself to the side just as the gun went off.

As he fell onto his side, Victor felt a blast of heat on the left side of his face. He wasn't shot, but he would feel the pain from the powder burn soon enough. He lay still in the weeds, his arms at his sides, the smell of the mud in his nostrils, trying not to breathe.

"I got him!" Doug shouted. "Hey, Trever, I got him!"

Victor could tell Doug was at least distracted, and probably wasn't paying any attention at all to him anymore. Slowly, he shifted his arm inside his jacket, to the small holster inside the waistline of his pants.

"Shut up!" Trever was saying. "Where is he?"

"He's right—" Doug started to say. He was turning to point to where Victor lay on the ground—

But Victor was sitting up now, with a small gun in his hands, pointed right at him.

Doug saw the gun in Victor's hand, and his eyes went wide. Immediately, he began to swing his own gun back toward Victor.

"Don't!" Victor said.

Doug's arm kept sweeping toward Victor, and his body began to crouch into a shooting stance.

"No!" Victor shouted.

The gun kept coming.

At the last possible instant, Victor squeezed the trigger. The sound from his gun was a tiny bang, but at the same moment, Doug's gun boomed again, the fire spitting out into the marsh a couple of feet to Victor's right.

Doug staggered backward, dropping the gun and putting

his hands to his chest. Within seconds, his steps became unsteady, then stopped, and he flopped into the reeds by the pool.

Victor climbed to his feet, grimacing with the pain of the powder burn. Doug was still twisting and groaning in pain, but Victor had seen men in that condition too many times, and they never lasted long. He turned his attention back to Trevor. He couldn't let him escape now. He had to finish it.

"Doug?" Trever called, and Victor could hear fear in his voice. "Was that you?"

Doug's movements grew still in the reeds. He probably wasn't quite dead yet, but he would not be answering anyone again.

Ducking low, Victor moved as silently as he could along the path toward Trever. He couldn't let Trever go, but shots had been fired, and men in uniform—or not—could start showing up at any moment.

"Doug?" Trever said again. "Are you there?"

Victor spotted Trever on the path, coming slowly back to where Doug had called him. As Trever approached, Victor crouched down and moved as far off the path as he could. He could feel his heart beating in his chest, shaking his whole body. He kept his gun at the ready. It wasn't a good firing position, but it was better than nothing. Somehow, Trever didn't hear or see him as he went by on the path back toward Doug.

"Doug?" Trever said again, quiet this time.

Victor stood up and stepped lightly back onto the path behind Trever, blocking his exit.

Trever, still unaware of Victor, spotted the body in the reeds. "Is that him, Doug?" he asked, the tone in his voice a mixture of hope and fear. "Doug, you got him?"

Victor crept silently down the path after Trever, his gun pointed at Trever's back. Unbelievably, he still didn't have a plan. He didn't want to merely shoot Trever in cold blood, but he didn't think it was going to come to that. Somehow.

Suddenly, the pitch of Trever's voice changed. "Doug?!" he said, not quite shouting. He hurried down the path, moving quicker the closer he got. He slid to a stop beside Doug, who had twisted onto his side, and pulled his arms to turn him over. "Oh, fuck, Doug!" he said, sounding close to tears.

"You should have confessed, Trever," Victor said as he stepped behind him.

Trever had pulled Doug's head into his lap, and he was keening and rocking back and forth.

"This is all because of you," Victor said.

"No," Trever said. He inhaled deeply and turned slightly toward Victor. "Everything was fine until you arrived." He gave Victor a bitter look. "Why did you have to come?"

"I had to come because everything was not fine for the kids at summer camp," Victor said, "and it was never going to be fine again for Kelsey French. But it didn't have to end this way." He scoffed in disgust. "You should have just confessed."

Trever, now brushing Doug's hair out of his face, turned to look at Victor. "I'm not gay, you know," he said.

"I don't care," Victor said.

"If you get out of here and I don't," Trever said, "I want you to tell them for me."

"No," Victor said. "Everybody's heard enough out of you. And besides," he added with a shake of his head, "no one is ever going to know I was here."

Suddenly, Trever raised his arm from the back side of Doug's head. He was holding Victor's gun.

He didn't get a chance to use it.

Victor fired once, and it was over.

CHAPTER TWENTY-FOUR

It was early Thursday evening when Victor knocked on Janine's door.

"Holy cow!" she said when she saw his face. "What happened?"

He gave her a grim smile. "I got very lucky," he said.

She rushed to him. "This is lucky?"

"Yes, it was," Victor said, "given what could have happened."

Janine tried to look closer at it. "Should we take you to the hospital?" she asked.

He shook his head, still with the stiff smile. "Can't," he said. "They would freak out."

"I'm sure they've seen worse," she said.

"I'm sure they have, too," Victor said, "but they would want to do paperwork, and I can't have that."

Janine drew back a bit and looked at him frowning in concern, and possibly understanding. "Well, come sit on my couch, then," she said. "Let me get you cleaned up."

She pulled him inside and tended to his face with cloths of warm water and antibiotic balm.

He got a hand mirror from her and looked at it. He had cleaned the bits of black gunpowder out of it in the bathroom of the motel, and the swelling had gone down some. In a day or so it might pass for a brush burn.

"Does it hurt?" she asked.

He shook his head. "Nothing ibuprofen can't handle."

She looked him up and down, worry on her face.

"I'm okay," he said, "but it's very good to be back."

She gave him a curious look. "Did you just get in?"

He nodded. He had left the grounds of the Trinity River Christian Outreach in a hurry, of course, after arranging the scene and erasing his tracks. On returning to the motel, he had cleaned himself up just enough to not attract attention, left the key on the nightstand, and headed back to the Greyhound station. Once back in St. Louis, he had come straight here. One reason was that, in his exhausted and sleep-deprived state, he wasn't the best person to be gauging the severity of the wound on his face. If it was bad enough to warrant medical attention, Janine would insist on it. The other reason was that, after the events in Dallas, he wanted to be in the presence of someone warm, and loving, and sane. He looked into Janine's eyes with a smile. He wished he could tell her more. Maybe he could someday. But probably not. Knowledge was a burden.

Seeing his smile, she shifted closer and leaned against him for a moment with her head on his shoulder, then tipped her face up to his. "Do you want to stay here tonight?" she asked.

He smiled. "I was thinking maybe we could stay at mine."

She raised her eyebrows. "Is it safe?" she asked.

He nodded.

"Nobody's looking for you?" she asked.

"No," he said, "not anymore."

She looked thoughtful for a moment, then turned back to him. "Wow," she said. "This is a milestone."

"I know," he said, his smile warming. "First time."

———

Friday morning, after Janine had showered and headed out to work, Victor called Angelina on the phone.

"I just dropped off the girls at school," she said. He could hear movement in the background. It sounded like she was out somewhere running an errand. "I only have a minute."

"It's okay," he said. He took a deep breath and narrowed his eyes. "I just wanted to tell you that you're right. It's time."

"Time for what?" she asked. Despite the early hour, she sounded exhausted, and he felt his heart go out to her.

"Time to move on," he said. He expected to feel more emotion at saying the words, and he was surprised that he didn't. It felt ... right.

Angelina was quiet on the phone, listening, thinking. "I know it is, Victor," she said. "It has been for a long time."

The tone of her statement almost invited a challenge, but Victor didn't go for it. He didn't want it to be right, but it was. "I guess so," he said.

"So, did you get the paperwork filled out?" she asked.

"Not yet, but I will soon," he said. The thought of filling out the paperwork was still repulsive to him. As much to himself as to her, he added, "I promise."

"Okay, thank you, Victor," she said. "I have to be go—"

"There's one thing, though," Victor said.

"What?"

"Can we not, you know, definitely decide that this is the end?"

She paused a moment. "What?"

"The divorce," he said. He took a deep breath. "It's the

right thing to do, but I don't want to say it's over *forever*. Just for now."

"What?" she said again, a hard edge coming into her voice. "That's the only kind there is."

"I know," Victor said, "but I just want to know that if, somewhere down the road, things change, and things are different again, more like they used to be, but different, the maybe ... we could ... you know." He took another quick breath. "Give it another try."

"Give ... what ... another try?" she asked. "Getting divorced? You mean changing the agreements? I don't know—"

"Not that," Victor said. "I mean *us*."

Angelina was quiet again, but Victor was relieved not to hear her groan. "I love you, Victor, and I'll probably always love you," she said finally, "but that's never going to happen."

———

Friday afternoon, with a little reluctance, Victor agreed to meet Lou at Maurice's. Victor got there early because he wanted a beer before talking to Lou. At least, for a change, he didn't feel irked by the people around him. At least, not to the degree that he needed to change their attitude. He did, though, make it *two* beers.

When Lou walked in and saw him already drinking, he said, "What are you doing? Are you pre-gaming me?"

Victor laughed. "*Pre*-gaming?" he said. "I'm still going from last time."

"Last time you were drinking coffee, champ," Lou said with a smile. He slid into the seat across from Victor and visibly flinched when he saw the mark on Victor's cheek. "What happened to your face?" he asked.

Victor shrugged. "I ran into a door frame," he said. "You know how clumsy I am."

"Door frame, huh?" Lou said. "Are you trying to tell me your new girlfriend is thumping on you? Is this your cry for help?"

Victor laughed. "Can't a guy get a brush burn without getting the third degree?" he asked. "What do you think? That I got shot in the face?"

Lou looked closer at him. "Not *in* the face, I'd say, but ..." His mouth made a tight line, and he added, "I've seen a lot of powder burns, and that looks like most of them."

Victor turned his face away and raised his hand to flag the waitress for another beer.

Lou sat back in his seat. "It sure looks like someone almost took your head off."

"Okay, okay," Victor said. "If I wanted the third degree, I'd call my ex-wife."

"Or you could call a cop," Lou said. "That should do it."

Victor shook his head, still turned away and flagging the waitress. "Is that what you wanted to see me for?" he asked.

"No, it isn't," Lou said. "This is about some *other* trouble that you got into. You remember your friend Jordan?"

Victor looked back at him. "Not my friend," he said.

"Yeah, I just thought from the way you kept going to see him ..." Lou said. "Anyway, it looks like he's going to take a plea deal and probably go away for a few years."

"What?" Victor said. "He's not going to fight it at trial and make the government prove their case?"

Lou shook his head with a knowing frown. "Like I told you, they always take a plea deal."

"Humph," Victor said. "I thought you told me they always hire the big guns."

Lou turned to him with a serious look. "Yeah," he said.

"That, too, but pretty often, the big guns tell them to take the deal."

"Well," Victor said, giving Lou a smile. "I hope it works out for him."

"Is that so?" Lou asked.

Victor nodded. "But enough about my drama. Whatever happened with that chop shop you were staking out?"

Lou shook his head in disgust. "It was legit," he said.

"What?" Victor said.

"That's why we don't like to take tips from the public," he said. "We saw they really were chopping up cars for parts, and we got a warrant and went in to bust them up, but it turned out to be just a bunch of college dropouts buying cars out of the junkyard and selling the parts online."

"Wow."

"I know," Lou said. "They said it was going to be the next billion-dollar big thing."

"No, I mean, 'wow, that investigation a pretty big fuck-up,'" Victor said.

"No, if someone gives us a tip, we have to follow up on it," Lou said.

Victor shrugged. "If you say so."

"Well, it isn't me that says so," Lou said. "The captain tells me, the chief tells him, the mayor tells him, and the public tells him. I'm just following orders."

Victor nodded. "That's the important thing," he said, sarcasm thick in his voice, "that nobody involved could be blamed for it."

Lou scoffed. "You're not wrong."

"Anyway," Victor said, "at least you got some free food out of it."

Lou nodded with a smile. "Yeah, and I'll take that any day."

———

Monday evening, Victor and Janine went to their ethics class together. By now, the burn on his face was almost gone, and nobody even noticed.

All anyone could talk about was Trever Mills anyway.

"Nobody knows what happened," Chandler said.

"What do you mean, nobody knows?" Jayson asked. "Trever and his 'friend' were found dead, each holding the gun that killed the other." He had used his fingers to put the word *friend* in air quotes.

"Yes, but nobody knows *why* they were found like that," Chandler said. "Nobody knows what led up to it, or how it transpired."

"People who live that lifestyle have the Devil in their hearts," Dapper Dan said. "So, in a very real way, the Devil did it."

Most of the class groaned, and Chandler turned away rolling his eyes.

"They said too Trever had given that Doug guy a bunch of money that day," Loretta said.

"Maybe the guy was blackmailing him," Janine said. "But they probably thought of that, right?"

"I didn't see that," Chandler said.

"They had something going on together," Jayson said. "Probably something no good."

Chandler was looking at Victor. "Do you have any thoughts about what might have happened, Mr. Storm?" he asked.

Victor thought for a moment, and for some reason the class went quiet and people turned to him, waiting for him to speak. "Well, I don't know anything about that Doug guy, so I'm not sure about him," he said at last, "but I'm very sure that Trever Mills got exactly what he deserved."

A murmur of agreement went through the class.

Chandler nodded, still regarding Victor carefully. "So do I," he said. "So do I."

———

In the beginning, his dreams were about his military missions. As he slept, his brain would rerun things that he did, but over which he had no control, moral dilemmas and mistakes.

Replaying them all, night after night, over and over.

Wishing things were different.

As time goes by, his dreams are less and less military, and more and more about moral dilemmas and mistakes of his own making.

In the dreams now, he sometimes sees young men trying too hard to grow mustaches.

Men who shouldn't have been there.

Mistakes now, of his own making.

Over and over.

———

Tuesday morning, after Janine went to work, Victor put on his shoes and his jacket and got on the bus. The trip was not very far, and he didn't have to check either the route or the schedule.

It was a familiar trip.

He got off the bus across the street from the VA hospital. Several other people got off at the same stop he did, and after they exited, most of them went to the crosswalk to continue on to it, but Victor stood by the bus stop with his hands in his pockets and stared across the street at the facility.

The sky was overcast and gray. Across the street at the VA

facility, between the sidewalk next to the street and the VA parking lot, was a thin strip of land filled with yellow, muddy grass and a few small saplings with thin, bare branches.

On the opposite side of the parking lot were the entry doors of the VA building. Victor saw a wide range of people coming and going, from crisp young men and women in a variety of uniforms, to grizzled old men with scars and limps, to men on crutches and in wheelchairs, to seasoned veterans with confident poses and serious faces.

Men like himself.

Kind of, anyway.

When the doors opened and closed, their black glass surfaces flashed gray as they reflected the overcast sky. It gave Victor the sense that, in a very real way, the world inside the building was different from the world outside it.

Watching the entrance to the VA building, Victor again had the sense that it was a whole different world inside. He realized, perhaps for the first time, that he *could* be part of that world.

But not today.

ABOUT THE AUTHOR

Born and raised in upstate New York, Terry F. Torrey has spent most of his adult life in Arizona with his amazing wife, awesome daughter, and remarkable cats. A lifelong learner, he was most pleased to complete the acclaimed Creative Writing program at Phoenix College.

Terry F. Torrey writes an eclectic variety of quirky, compelling, and heartfelt books and shorts, including campy but realistic pop-culture monster novels, page-turning vigilante action novels, riveting suspense novels with shades of noir, cozy upstate campus mysteries, clean contemporary westerns, and sharp works of political satire.

Find all of Terry F. Torrey's writings at terryftorrey.com.